He flicked on the one single bulb that hung in the center of the room. Light reflected back at him from hundreds of glass bottles and jars that lined the shelves. Each contained a substance deemed illegal by the great state of Oklahoma. If anyone found this room, he'd be in jail for a long time, and while it was not the worst thing he'd done in his life, it was what brought him the most joy.

Ezekiel sighed, wiping the dirt from the knees of his pants. Every shelf held enough booze to keep the county drunk for at least a week. But he saw dollar signs, not alcohol, and he knew he had a lot of work to do before the election.

Praise for Nicholas Lyon

First place winner of the 2019 Oklahoma Writers Federation, Inc., Historical Fiction Novel category.

The Baptist Bootlegger

by

Nicholas Lyon

This is a work of fiction. Names, characters, places, and incidents are either the product of the author's imagination or are used fictitiously, and any resemblance to actual persons living or dead, business establishments, events, or locales, is entirely coincidental.

The Baptist Bootlegger

Contact Information: info@thewildrosepress.com

Cover Art by *Jennifer Greeff*

The Wild Rose Press, Inc.
PO Box 708
Adams Basin, NY 14410-0708
Visit us at www.thewildrosepress.com

Publishing History
First Edition, 2022
Trade Paperback ISBN 978-1-5092-4599-4
Digital ISBN 978-1-5092-4600-7

Published in the United States of America

Dedication

To Mom and Dad - For taking me to church and showing me God.

Chapter 1

Ezekiel

Ezekiel Wilson, preacher at the First Baptist Church, sat behind his desk and contemplated the idea that there might be another moonshiner in town. That could be a problem, not only for his flock, but for him. He would have to do some digging.

In that small Oklahoma town there were only two kinds of people: those going to Heaven and those going to Hell. That was the idea that the First Baptist Church preacher, Ezekiel Wilson, liked to impart on his congregation, though he didn't believe a word of it himself.

In the pulpit each week, he worked them over, reminding them that at any moment the devil could consume their very souls. The passionate delivery usually resulted in a large amount of knees bending in prayer before the altar.

People still talked about the first time they ever heard Brother Ezekiel preach back in 1946. He'd come to this small church, his first assignment, with not much more than the suit on his back and the Bible in his hand. But when he stood in the pulpit, it was as if the good Lord had been right behind him, shouting those words through him. There had been a revival that day and church didn't let out until nine o'clock that night. In all thirty-five people were saved and twice as many had recommitted their lives to the Lord.

Ezekiel's favorite place in the church was his office; the leather-backed armchair brought a sense of comfort not unlike a warm hug from loving arms. Unfortunately, the office made him easily accessible. A quick knock at the door and Mike Arrington brought some of the cool fall air in with him when he entered. The preacher had to fight the urge to roll his eyes at the arrival of his head deacon.

"Why, hello, Brother Mike," Ezekiel said, slipping easily into the role of friendly minister. "What brings you in today?"

Mike plucked at his thin, salt and pepper mustache, a gesture reserved for his most anxious moments. His eyes, amplified in their size by his glasses, seemed even larger today. "Did you see the paper this morning?"

"I have not." Ezekiel rubbed at his cheek, thinking about what could possibly be in the paper. "Hopefully there's nothing too disconcerting there."

Mike dropped the hand from his mustache and leaned forward. "Well, it seems the thing that I've been dreading above all other things may be coming to fruition."

"You mean the Devil is coming to Oklahoma?"

"It is the Devil as far as I'm concerned, the Devil in liquid form."

Ezekiel's eyes grew round, causing his brown irises to get lost in the sea of white. "You don't mean...*alcohol*?" The last word came out barely above a whisper, as if the word itself could burst into flame in the preacher's office.

"Yes, I do. They're talking about making it legal,

putting the vote to the people again. That means that any man could just go to the store and buy sin by the bottle anytime he wanted to and no one can stop him."

Ezekiel fumbled with the rubber band around his own newspaper. Heart racing, he scanned the text before him. "This can't be happening." His mind and attention focused solely on the newspaper story in front of him; he forgot for the moment that Mike was in the room. This was not the first time that Oklahomans had voted to repeal prohibition in the state and ratify the Twenty-First Amendment. Deep down, he believed that this wouldn't be the last time. Here he'd been merely worried about a bootlegger in town, when soon he could be worrying about the whole state being overrun.

Silence settled in the office while Ezekiel perused the paper. Eventually, Mike spoke up, "Surely you can do something about this, can't you?"

Ezekiel's unfocused gaze came to settle on the deacon's face. "I don't know that I can. Some things are even beyond me. We'll have to inform the prayer chain and get them started. And I can guarantee I know what I'll be preaching come this Sunday."

Mike smiled. "I knew you would have an answer." The morning sunshine tumbled down through the blinds, casting the scene into a chopped combination of shadow and light.

"I thought we had more time." Ezekiel's downcast eyes once more focused on the newsprint that lay on his desk.

With the slightest hint of timidity in his voice, Mike said, "Do you think there is already alcohol here?"

The preacher's eyes shot up. "Here?" He fought the urge to chuckle and once more played Mike's gullibility.

"Why would that question even enter your mind? What have you to gain from thinking along such an evil path?"

"Well, it's just that since Kansas legalized it ten years ago, wouldn't it be easy for someone to sneak it back across the state line?"

Ezekiel rubbed his hand across his chin. "I suppose it would simply be a matter of someone really wanting to do that. Obviously the national prohibition was a failure, so we're not able to keep all of it out. I would guess that, yes, there are plenty who are able to get it on their own."

Mike settled back in his chair and crossed his legs. Ezekiel watched him process the information. Ezekiel knew Mike well enough to know about his estranged uncle who'd nearly killed himself with homemade moonshine, an anecdote Mike always brought up whenever he had the chance. To Ezekiel, Mike was the perfect representation of the sinner casting the first stone.

"There's nothing to it, Mike. I'll have to battle from the pulpit and you'll have to battle on the streets. Can you organize a door-to-door flier?"

"Sure, I can." He uncrossed his legs and leaned forward. "We've got at least twenty families who would help us tonight." He tapped the desk with his index finger to punctuate the sentence.

"Good, good. Then we need to begin this work if we're ever going to stop these horrid ideas."

Mike stood to go, but Ezekiel stopped him. "Brother Mike, thank you for bringing this to my attention. Shall we pray before you go?"

"Indeed."

They grabbed hands like old friends and Ezekiel led them in prayer.

After the prayer, Ezekiel was once more alone with his thoughts. He was sure that his fellow Oklahomans would do the right thing and vote down the bill again, but something kept nagging at him.

He pulled his tie from his neck and left it on his desk. He rolled up his sleeves and stepped from his office.

"Wanda," he called to his secretary, "I'm going to step out for lunch."

She waved that she'd heard, clearly busy putting together the Sunday bulletin and not wanting to be distracted. He turned from her and wandered down the hall of the offices of the church. He paid no attention to the youth pastor or the music minister, both pretending to do work in their own offices.

He stepped outside into bright sunlight. His house, the parsonage, stood only twenty feet from the back door of the church. He didn't break stride as he walked up the slight driveway reserved for deliveries and drop-offs. He entered his house through the back door and made his way down the stairs to the darkened basement.

The house was quite large, big enough for a family of four or five with a complete living space downstairs. He didn't need that much space, but the church insisted that he live there for free, so he took advantage of it.

He crossed the main room of the basement and stood before the east wall. It was covered in a pale green wall paper that badly needed replacing. One portion right above where he stood had been torn. He'd done that himself. The false wall he'd built blended in too well to the surrounding wall. The tear helped him find it.

He pushed it to one side to reveal a low earthen tunnel. Wooden joists every few feet insured it wouldn't collapse. He crawled to a room just below the alley beside his house. He flicked on the one single bulb that hung in the center of the room. Light reflected back at him from hundreds of glass bottles and jars that lined the shelves. Each contained a substance deemed illegal by the great state of Oklahoma. If anyone found this room, he'd be in jail for a long time, and while it was not the worst thing he'd done in his life, it was what brought him the most joy.

Ezekiel sighed, wiping the dirt from the knees of his pants. Every shelf held enough booze to keep the county drunk for at least a week. But he saw dollar signs, not alcohol, and he knew he had a lot of work to do before the election.

Chapter 2

Robert

The straw poked and scratched as Robert lifted the bales, but he barely noticed. He smiled as he worked, even hummed a little. Two things caused the smile: the pleasant weather and the Fall Festival. The hayride, a part of the annual Fall Festival, was always one of the most popular events and this year, he would get to drive the truck. His dad, Mike, had finally agreed that he was old enough. However, that also meant that Mike expected him to load the trailer on his own today.

Still, Robert enjoyed the work because he would enjoy the reward. He hoped that he would finally be able to impress Becky. Rebecca Lewis was the kind of girl most teenage guys dreamed of, with hair so blonde it was almost white and a personality so sweet it made her exorbitant outward beauty almost sour by comparison. It was her eyes, however, that haunted him the most. The dark blue that poured forth from the black irises tingled the depths of his soul. And while he could spend hours with her in his mind, she never quite gave him a chance.

He lifted another bale and thought of Becky's eyes. He started humming "Everyday" by Buddy Holly, the words reflecting Robert's deep desires for Becky. Robert's dad didn't allow him to listen to rock n' roll, but he had all of Buddy Holly's 45s hidden in a box under his bed, and his mom liked them almost as much as he did.

It was the first bit of rebellion Robert had.

Becky was restless, and even as a boy of seventeen, Robert could see that she might be his downfall. Still, he didn't care. If a fall from grace meant he got to kiss her lips, even once, that was enough for him, a thought that terrified and excited him.

"Robert, are you about finished over there?" His father's voice jolted him back from the edges of that fall. He moved like a scared rat as he threw another bale of hay on the trailer.

"Yes, sir. I've got maybe three to go."

"Good. When you're finished with that, run into town and pick up some flour so your ma can make some bread." Mike Arrington didn't make requests of his son; he gave demands.

"Weren't you in town earlier?" The words were out before he could stop them. He'd been in the sun too long with images of Becky entangling the careful workings of his brain.

"What did you say?"

Robert lifted another bale, prepared himself, and took a breath. It was too late now. "I just thought you were in town earlier."

Mike stalked over to Robert and peered at him. Despite the fact that Robert stood five inches higher than his dad, he still cowered before that gaze.

"What I did earlier doesn't matter to you." His hand flew out and cuffed Robert's cheek. To his credit, Robert kept hold of the bale of hay and barely made a sound of surprise at the slap. If he had seen Mike with Brother Ezekiel earlier, he would believe it to be a different man than the one standing in front of him. "Once you're finished," Mike said, "you can go get your mother that flour. After dinner, you'll stay in your room." He turned back toward the house, and as he opened the front door, he added, "I'll drive the truck tonight."

The door slapped closed in its frame, a sound eerily similar to Mike slapping his son. Robert stared at the house and fought the tears threatening to stream down his cheeks. It was unfair, just like so much of his life. The tingles in his cheek became a distant memory. He tried to push away the image of Becky's eyes now; he wouldn't be seeing them after all. He threw the bale of hay he'd been holding onto the truck and sighed. Every Sunday morning and every Sunday night they made their way to town to attend the First Baptist Church services. Wednesday nights, Robert was required to attend the youth group. He learned about God, grace, and sacrifice. He learned about forgiveness. But most importantly, he learned about sin, and he wondered how his dad could be in those church services with him and never learn the same things.

The other work truck pulled up beside him and Charles got out of the cab. He lifted the hat off his head and ran a hand over his cropped blond hair.

"What's wrong, boy?" His voice still carried some of that Australian accent that he'd attempted to lose in the five years since coming to America.

Robert resented the way someone just six years older than him could call him "boy." "I told you not to call me that." He threw another bale on the trailer, not caring how it landed.

"I know you did. You better hurry with those hay bales or they'll cancel the ride."

Robert sighed. "I wish it was canceled." He tossed another on.

"And why would you say that?"

"I'm not allowed to drive now." He tilted his head back toward the house. "He won't let me." He tried to keep the pain out of his voice, but still he felt the sting of the tears in the corners of his eyes.

"I'm not even surprised you did something to piss him off, but I hope it was worth it."

"Of course it wasn't." Robert lifted the last hay bale and threw it on the trailer. "I just wanted to impress a girl." His cheeks burned hot at the revelation.

Charles smiled at him. "What kind of girl is that?"

"Kind? Well, the best kind, I suppose. She's beautiful and sweet. I just don't know that she's ever going to notice me."

Charles stared at him, letting the smile stay on his face. He had previously pressed conversations toward topics that were not easy for Baptist boys to hear. Today, he pushed a little further. "You should go anyway. That'll impress the girl."

Robert smiled in spite of the terrifying new turn the conversation took. "I don't think that disobeying my father would impress this girl very much." He rubbed his hands on his jeans and shifted his weight from foot to foot.

Charles shrugged. "If that's what you want to believe. But trust me when I tell you this: girls love rebels." He pointed at Robert. "That could be you, my friend. Who else has something to rebel against like you?"

Robert didn't respond, but stared down at the dirt like he always did when Charles steered the conversations into exciting and terrifying territories. It brought out the same excitement in him that he supposed God brought out of the diehard Baptists at his church.

Charles let the silence spin out before adding, "Hey, boy, why don't you take the work truck after your father leaves and see if you can find your girl? The worst that could happen is you get caught. Things might be pretty bad for a couple days if that happens, but the Bible does speak of forgiveness."

Robert caught Charles' eye and smiled. And though his burning cheeks framed the smile, it still revealed his rebellious nature that he longed to tap into. Things, he felt, needed to change.

Chapter 3

Ezekiel

The booze bottles and jars glared back at him, reflecting the single overhead light bulb, accusing him of inaction. Ezekiel'd been down here in his secret room for the better part of an hour. Upstairs he heard the telephone ring a few times, probably Wanda wondering where he'd gone. He didn't care. All he cared about was the money he saw in front of him. The liquid gold resting in all this glass could finance his church for another three years if he could sell it at the current market rate. He wouldn't have to ask for donations for a long time.

The text from the paper and Mike Arrington's smug face floated back into his mind. He had to figure something out. Sure, he could preach against booze, but he did that a lot anyway. He was, after all, Baptist. He felt like there had to be something more to this. He had to ensure that the people of his town knew that Repeal was a dangerous road, a road so littered with traps and landmines that their lives would never be the same. He trusted in the Oklahomans' desire to continue to buy booze tax free.

"Something has to be done," he muttered. Finally, with one last look around the room, he crawled back out of the tunnel and replaced the fake wall. He would use his resources. He would initiate the prayer chain. He would not be lazy in the coming days of this war. He would mobilize his underlings, the ones who had no idea who they worked for, who sold the booze on the streets for him.

Back in his office, ignoring Wanda's questions and the ridiculous amount of phone calls he'd gotten during lunch, he sat at his desk and got to work. First he called every one of his deacons. Some of them were at work, but some he managed to catch at lunch. He didn't bother calling Mike Arrington, it would only lead to another lengthy discussion if he answered. If Mike didn't answer, well, Lucy was probably home.

He couldn't think about her right now.

One of the other deacons, an older man by the name of Dale, seemed so concerned with the prospect of Repeal that he immediately began drafting a flier to pass around to the town with the hopes of educating "the lost," as he called them. The pride that Ezekiel had come to know and nourish swelled. He knew that if anyone could stop this bulldozer from destroying what he'd built, it would be the people from his congregation, his flock.

That night, after a day full of spreading fliers around town, making phone calls, and even meeting with some of the other preachers in town over dinner to discuss the upcoming vote, Ezekiel lay on his couch and attempted to keep his eyes open long enough to see the evening news. The black and white images danced across his vision, and he felt a dreary sense of unreality as he stared at them.

The phone in his kitchen rang and pulled him back out of the well of sleep he'd been falling into.

"Hello," he said into the receiver.

"Boss, I just ran into Billy West. He's drunk."

"Well, that's good, isn't it?" Ezekiel shook his head to clear the sleep from it.

"It would be if he was buying from us. Unfortunately, there seems to be someone else making it in town again."

Ezekiel's knuckles turned white, the blood squeezed out of them. "Who would dare?" Ezekiel whispered. He'd spent the whole day thinking about what would happen if Repeal passed, and never considered that someone else could be supplying his town with booze they should be buying from him.

"I'm not sure, boss. Billy just went home. Want me to go visit him?"

Typically, Ezekiel didn't handle the dirty work. He preferred people to still believe he was the preacher he claimed to be on Sunday mornings, but the anger got the better of him. "I'll go. You hang tight. I'll call if I need anything."

The voice on the other end began to protest, but Ezekiel slammed the phone back into its cradle. He took one last long glance at his couch and the sleep he'd nearly found there then stormed out the door.

****

The summer of 1946, a good thirteen years before prohibition would end in Oklahoma, Ezekiel Wilson had just finished his seminary courses, graduated with good marks, and sent his résumé all over the state. He wanted to preach and couldn't wait for it.

The first, and what would turn out to be the only Call, came in the middle of July. A small church in the northwest part of the state wanted him to come In View of a Call, as the Baptists called it. They'd already spoken to his references, his professors, the ones he'd put on the list, and they had said great things about him. He couldn't wait to share the news.

That night he went by Mary's place. She lived in Shawnee, just down the street from the University. He still lived on campus, but it was close enough that he could walk. He'd never been to her house after the sun had gone down.

"I finally got the call," he said to her, his heart jumping all through his chest like a fumbled football.

Mary, her dark hair pulled back and exhaustion painting her pretty face, let loose a "Whoop!" that echoed through the streets. The smile and elation on her face nearly made the years in seminary worth it to Ezekiel.

"Will you go with me?" he asked once their embrace had ended.

She stepped back from him, her eyes searching his. The hot summer air swirling around them on her small porch. "Do you mean it?" she asked. Mixing with the excitement was the nervousness he'd seen before when he mentioned marriage. He loved Mary and expected nothing less than to grow old with her. To prove it, he fell to one knee and pulled out the ring his grandmother had worn. The dainty diamond diverted the attention from the simple golden band. He'd gotten it from his mother three months earlier and had been waiting for the right moment.

"Oh, Ezekiel!" Her hands covered her mouth and tears spilled down her cheeks.

"Will you marry me?" he asked.

With a celebration in mind, Mary invited Ezekiel into her house where she proceeded to make dinner for them. She also made enough for her two housemates, young girls who had just started college the year before. Their parents set up the living arrangement with Mary in the hopes that she could be a good influence on the girls. And she was.

The two girls, Daphne and Sally, came into the kitchen and hugged Mary and squealed at the sight of the ring. It was common for girls to go to college with the hopes of getting just such a ring.

Before eating Ezekiel said the easiest blessing he'd ever said in his life. He prayed for the nourishment his body would receive, but mostly he thanked God for his future bride and for the celebration of life before them.

"So you're going to take good care of our girl, right, Ezekiel?" Daphne asked between bites of spaghetti.

"You know it." His smile said everything about how he felt at that moment. All of his life was finally coming together and he couldn't think of a better person to spend it with. "The only problem, of course, is that you two will have to find a new roommate."

Sally's fork froze halfway to her mouth. "I hadn't thought of that, Mary. When do you think you'll be leaving?"

Mary grabbed her hand. "Don't worry about that right now. You guys will be taken care of, I swear."

When it came time to get married and move, Mary had found the perfect roommate to take her place. Ezekiel carried the final box out of the house, with Mary following closely behind. "This is the end of my life in Shawnee," she said.

Ezekiel smiled. "But this is just the beginning."

Chapter 4

Nigel

"Grab your gear!" the captain barked. Instantly, the room jumped into action. Cops ran back and forth around the room, grabbing guns, grabbing ammo, some even grabbed helmets like they were storming the beaches of Normandy. Inspector Nigel Baxter leapt to his feet, throwing his hat on his head and checking his side piece once more for ammo. He didn't plan on firing his gun, but he would be ready if he had to.

"I need every one of you," the captain continued to shout over the heads of the officers as they gathered in front of him. "We have found the location of a notorious alcohol dealer in Oklahoma City, and we are going to get him tonight. We don't know how many people may be there, but we won't give them the chance to take shelter. We have to take him down." He locked eyes with Nigel. "Inspector, you're with me. Now, everyone, move out."

The officers filed out, rifles in hand. For some, this was the first exciting thing that had happened in their short careers as police officers. Nigel knew that for many, it would be the last.

He stepped up next to the captain. "Is it Tommy Hickey?"

"You know it," the captain responded with a gleam in his eye. Captain Roger Harris was a solid man, built, many believed, entirely out of bricks. A rock-hard, four inches taller than Nigel, he was someone to look up to both figuratively and literally.

Nigel Baxter had been pursuing leads for months trying to track down this notorious gangster in the Oklahoma City area. Where there was a boom in alcohol sales, drunken parties, intoxicated citizens, Nigel was sure Hickey had been there. He could not find the man; it was like trying to nail water to the wall. And now it seemed, some sort of lucky break would give someone else the credit. Recognition would be nice, but really Nigel wanted to take this man down. While Oklahoma police and politicians mostly ignored the prohibition laws that had been in effect for fifty years, it was a whole different story when someone went out of their way to get the attention of the police. Nigel had made it his personal mission to catch Thomas Hickey.

The sirens howled as the cars flew down toward the warehouse district. It was dark on this side of the city at night, and Nigel could see plenty of vagabonds wandering with all of their worldly possessions as they moved on down the road. The captain's car pulled up in front of one of the many warehouses down here, the headlights bounding back off of the red brick building. Nigel jumped out of the car before it had the chance to come to a complete stop. He followed the captain as he made his way to the door in the side of the building, a small yellow light casting it's pall over the area, insects bouncing around the bulb. The other police cars piled in around the captain's car and the red lights beat the area in their steady rhythm.

The door to the warehouse burst open before Nigel and Harris could make it. Tommy Hickey stepped out of the darkened interior of the warehouse, pushing a woman in front of him. Her eyes were wide and terrified as Hickey pressed the muzzle of his gun into the side of her neck. Her eyes found Nigel's and he could see the pleading there, but that was not his current concern. The man holding the gun had the wild look of a predator caught in a trap, his hair stuck out at all angles, his face hadn't been shaved, and his shirt probably started life as white, but it was hard to tell now in its current state. Nigel had dreamed of this, of taking down the man who had long haunted these streets. And here he stood with a hostage.

"Hickey," Captain Harris said, "you won't be leaving here alive if you decide to do this. Let the girl go and let us arrest you. Going to jail for a while is better than the alternative."

"You guys come here with your guns and you expect me to go quietly?" Hickey responded, his voice as wild as his hair. "All I ever did was supply some alcohol to people who wanted it. I wasn't hurting anyone."

"You're breaking the law," Nigel said. The presence of the officers behind him helped him to feel a little more confident.

The woman didn't struggle as Hickey held her, but her eyes were like wild alley cats, darting from Harris to Nigel. *This will not end well*, Nigel thought. That was when Hickey fired his gun. Captain Harris hit the ground at the sound, but Nigel pulled his own weapon from its holster. The woman drifted to the ground, a gaping wound in her neck, eyes no longer darting. Nigel ran forward, closing the distance between himself and Hickey before the woman's body hit the ground. Hickey brought the gun, hot as it was, to the side of his head, but

Nigel was there before he could fire. Hickey and Nigel hit the ground in a heap.

Chapter 5

Ezekiel

Brother Ezekiel perched himself on a couch waiting for one of his less faithful. Billy West had not been expecting company, so he moved slower getting them refreshments.

The stink in the tight living room suggested neglect rather than straight filth. Every surface collected at least an inch of dust including the couch where Ezekiel Wilson sat. He tried to move little so as to avoid disturbing anything and sending more clouds of dust into the air.

Ezekiel decided that Billy West must not remember that this room was even a part of the house. Indeed, it was Ezekiel's first time in his churchgoer's living room as they usually met in the breakfast nook of his kitchen around a yellowed table with cracked vinyl chairs. But tonight, he needed to be a little more official, and so he chose the dusty living room.

"Might need a little dusting in here, Billy," Ezekiel called to him. He could just see Billy through the door preparing two glasses of iced tea, unsweetened. The man jumped at the sound of Ezekiel's voice.

Ezekiel licked his lips and thought about the other times he'd been to see Billy. The man was a good churchgoer, but usually came with a hangover. Ezekiel considered him one of his most reliable alcoholics, and yet, when he came to visit it was to discuss how Billy could get help staying away from the booze. But tonight, Ezekiel had to know where he was getting the booze.

As he entered the room, holding to the two glasses of tea, Billy West took a shaking breath. "Here you are, Brother."

Ezekiel took the glass and drank deeply. He smacked his lips before saying, "I thank you. You know, it's taken me quite some time to adjust to drinking tea this way, but now that I do, I can't go back. Too much sugar really isn't good for a man."

Billy drank from his own glass and said nothing in response. The ice in his glass clanked against the sides.

"Sometimes though, we like something a little stronger than just tea, don't we, Billy?" He took another drink, not bothering to see what kind of effect his words had on his sheep.

"I, uh, guess that I, uh, don't really have any idea what you could be referring to." He tried to take another drink of his own tea, but his hand shook so severely that he ended up spilling it down his chin.

A gospel song warbled on the cheap turntable Billy had in his kitchen. He liked to play gospel songs for Ezekiel to prove his good Christian heritage. Personally, Ezekiel would have preferred one of his Elvis 45s that Billy pretended he didn't have.

He cleared his head and reminded himself why he was in Billy's living room in the first place. The anger came roaring back like a mountainous tidal wave gearing up to destroy the coastline. He took one final drink, stood, and hurled the glass against the wall. Pieces of glass and ice flecked with tea sailed around the room.

The movement happened with such surety, Ezekiel could have been simply stretching his arms.

"What's goin' on?" The words came from Billy's throat involuntarily as he ducked to avoid any glass that might catch him. He spilled the rest of his tea in the process.

"What do you mean, 'What's goin' on?' I have a problem, Billy West, and it starts," he jabbed the man in the forehead with a thin, sharp index finger, "right between those thick eyebrows of yours. Can you understand what I'm saying?"

Tears slipped down Billy's quivering face. His eyes dipped down and away from Ezekiel then popped back up to land somewhere on Ezekiel's face. It obviously pained this man, this sinner, this sheep to look at his shepherd. A sob escaped his trembling lips.

Ezekiel lowered his voice, bringing his anger back into check. "Now tell me where you're getting your stuff."

Billy nodded, the tremble not leaving his lips, however, a new wave of confidence came over him. "Oh, is that it?" he asked. "Well, I get some stuff at the grocery, sometimes, at the hardware store. I don't know what kind of stuff you mean, sir."

This time it wasn't just an index finger that caught Billy in the forehead, but the whole fist. Billy fell out of the chair and sprawled on the ground with a moan, his own tea glass broke with the impact on the floor. If Ezekiel kept this up, he'd have to bring his own glass next time.

Ezekiel pulled a handkerchief out the breast pocket of his suit coat and mopped his sweaty face with it. He wished he had more tea.

"Now, Billy, I'm through with these games. You and I both know that you've got a supplier of hooch, that you have it somewhere in your house, and I want to know where it is and who got it for you."

A dawn of understanding crept into Billy's upturned eyes. God, Ezekiel thought, he really is dumb. Billy rubbed furiously at his forehead. "I-I finished my last jar this morning."

"You at least seem to be understanding what I am saying. Now tell me, where did you get it?"

"I guess I bought it myself."

Ezekiel couldn't take the stupid answers. He tried to remain calm, but the events of the day brought his anger ever closer to the surface. He stood so close to finding this secret moonshiner in town so he could take him out, and Billy stood mute. His fist found Billy's face again, this time just an inch or two lower. Blood spurted from the poor fool's nose and Ezekiel had to remind himself not to enjoy this too much and not to go too far.

The drunk grabbed his nose. "Why'd you hit me?"

Ezekiel sighed. "Jesus Christ died on a cross to bear your sins, and here you are continuing to live in that sin. A bleeding nose and a sore head are nothing compared to your soul roasting forever in Hell." He sat in a chair next to the poor sap. "Now, tell me where you get it, so we can end this debauchery." He liked to use big words with Billy because it confused the man.

"Why couldn't I drive into Kansas and buy my own? It's not so far."

"I suppose you could." Ezekiel stood once more, unbuttoned his coat, pulled it off, and rolled up his sleeves. "I don't believe that, and I know you don't either."

Billy's eyes widened as Ezekiel bore down on him. He saw real fear and it fueled his anger even more. Billy held his hands over his head. "Okay," he shouted, "I don't buy it in Kansas. I get it down the street from Hank Thomas. He's been making it in the shed behind his house. Just don't hit me again." Billy sobbed, snot mingling with the blood spilling from his nose.

"Hank? That old bastard?" Hank Thomas didn't go to his church, or any church that Ezekiel knew about, but that didn't stop him from knowing him. He'd only been in town for a couple of years and had attempted several different careers that never seemed to pan out. And here he was, starting another one. Ezekiel placed a hand on Billy's shoulder. "Now that wasn't so hard, Billy, was it?"

"You won't tell him it was me who told, will you?"

"If it will free you from your sins, I would publish it in the paper tomorrow." Ezekiel unrolled his sleeves and buttoned the cuffs.

Billy wiped at the tears in his eyes and Ezekiel handed him the handkerchief to dab at the blood on his face. "I worry about you, Billy. Why can't you give up the drink?"

"I don't know, pastor, but I sure wish I did."

"Now, you'll be in church on Sunday, won't you? I'll be doing a special sermon for anyone who thinks ending prohibition is a good idea."

"That's good, sir, that's real good, but I'm not one of those. I don't want prohibition to end."

"Really? And why would that be? You clearly like the booze."

"Well, sir, I am afraid with it being readily available and completely legal, I would fall deeper into it. I'm barely hanging on as it is." The blood stained the handkerchief and Ezekiel knew it would never be clean again.

Ezekiel nodded; it was actually one of the sanest reasons he'd heard to keep prohibition. Clearly, though, he didn't care for Billy West's sobriety, only that he wanted to reap the benefits of his addiction.

"Do you believe that Hank Thomas is home at the moment?" Ezekiel grabbed his coat and slid into it with the practiced grace of a ballroom dancer sliding into a waltz.

"I wouldn't really know, sir. I had hoped so. I was hoping to get some more hooch before you came by and reminded me of the straight and narrow path that I should be on." He nodded furiously at the end of his statement as if to make Ezekiel believe in his redemption.

"Yes, thank you, Billy. You're a great help. Sorry about the glass, but thanks for the tea."

"I never liked that glass anyway."

"Sure, you did. It was wrong of me to smash it. Here," he pulled a wad of cash out of the inside pocket of his suit. It was one-dollar bills, so it looked like a lot, but amounted to little. "Take this. You can replace it."

"You don't have to do that," Billy said as he put the money in his pocket. That was a little quirk that Ezekiel enjoyed about most people: they would deny needing the money as they took it. The world was a queer place, he had once decided, any place that could allow a Baptist preacher to bootleg booze was indeed a queer place.

He walked out of Billy West's house with Billy still saying some of the babble he'd been saying since Ezekiel had put the fear of God in him. He ignored Billy's words, and stepped gingerly around the junk in the front yard.

He climbed into the driver's side of his black Chevrolet and was not surprised to see his right-hand man in the passenger seat.

"Johnny, didn't I tell you I'd call if I needed you?"

A deep and luxurious voice, like deep velvet, responded. "Sure you did, boss, but when has that stopped me?"

Ezekiel laughed. "That's why I always like you, Johnny, you never listen."

He started the car and pulled away from the curb. "It seems we have another booze supplier in town that we'll need to visit with. We've got to get this under control before others start believing that it's okay to make and sell their own. I've got so much in my basement, if Repeal happens, I'm going to be stuck with a liquid fortune that nobody wants to buy anymore."

"Sure, boss, I'll go talk to him. Maybe he'll work for you, cut you in."

"In a perfect world. But just in case, you'll need to be ready."

"Sure, boss. You going to the Festival tonight?"

"Damn." Ezekiel slapped the wheel of the car. "I forgot that it was tonight. Guess I'll park at my house and mosey on over there. You head over to Hank's house. And take a gun, Johnny."

"You don't have to worry about that."

Ezekiel parked at his house and barely glanced at Johnny as he walked away from the church. With another longer glance at his house and the couch where he almost found rest, Ezekiel headed off to the north and toward the sounds of the Fall Festival.

Chapter 6

Nigel

The other officers in the building all treated Nigel with a different sort of respect after he took down Hickey. Everyone knew his name and patted him on the shoulder as he walked by. He probably wouldn't need to buy a cigar again as long as his boys in blue were around.

Back in the office, he sat at his desk and tried to understand the illegal booze statistics he'd tracked down. His blue sport coat hung over the back of his chair, the most casual he allowed himself to be at work. He kept his shirt buttoned to the top and his tie tight. And he was one of the only men in the precinct to sport cufflinks. Those along with his pencil-thin mustache made him that much more dapper.

"Hey, Nigel…"

He chose to ignore the voice beside his desk. Instead, he focused more closely on the data in front of him.

With burning cheeks, the young man tried again, "Uh, Inspector Baxter?"

Nigel laid his papers aside, stifled a sigh, and bore his eyes into the officer.

"Did you see the news about the Vote?" the young officer said.

Nigel could actually hear the capital letter in the way

the officer said the word vote. He approached the idea with such reverence. Nigel wanted to continue to work, but he also enjoyed giving his opinion when it was sought. "It won't pass," Nigel said. "Don't get your hopes up. We're going to be in a dry state on the books until they decide to do something about it on the streets. We do our job, but what does it matter to arrest a drunk and have him back out in a few hours?"

The young man nodded, mouth hanging open like a window on a spring day.

"That's how flies get in," Nigel said.

"Huh?" The mouth snapped shut.

"Nothing at all, nothing at all."

Nigel waited for a moment, wondering if the officer would say something more, maybe share his own opinion, but he just stood there. Nigel let his eyes drop back down to the papers he'd been reading. It was a small report on some of the more notorious places where alcohol could be found in the state. It was not hard to get a clear sign that prohibition had indeed failed. However, if it became legal again, taxes would drive the cost way up, and his fellow Oklahomans did not want that.

The state had been a "dry" state since it first came into the Union in 1907, and like the national prohibition, it hadn't worked. However, when the United States government passed the Twenty-First Amendment, Oklahoma was one of the states that did not ratify it. The state government gave in a little by allowing "suds," a non-intoxicating 3.2 percent beer. When the surrounding states began to allow alcohol sales, Oklahoma couldn't keep it out of the state. Repeated attempts were made to legalize it, but all had failed.

Personally, Nigel Baxter never touched the stuff in

his home state. Being an officer of the law meant that he must obey the laws, at least that's how he felt. In other states, however, there were no laws against drinking, so when the opportunity took him to another place, he accepted opportunity's favor and drank himself silly.

What brought Nigel back to the figures in his hand over and over was that it didn't quite make sense. The obvious place to find booze was in central Oklahoma, not because it was easiest to get to from surrounding states, but because of the largest population. The second was around Tulsa. But another portion of the state had numbers almost as high as the state's biggest cities.

He cleared some papers off the map of Oklahoma he'd taped to the top of his desk. Using a red pen, he circled the northwest part of the state and tapped the area in the middle of it a few times, his mind busy with attempting to understand. "What is happening here?" he whispered.

There was a college there, which might explain some of it, sure, but not that much. Never that much. Just looking at the numbers made it seem that there was no prohibition in northwest Oklahoma. He furrowed his brow and scratched at his not insignificant nose.

"Who d'you like for governor?" a voice asked. Though northwest Oklahoma had his attention, when it came to politics, Nigel could be distracted quite easily. Two officers stood near his desk, discussing the upcoming election for governor. Usually, Nigel only had to deal with the detectives in the Oklahoma City Police Station, but for some reason, today beat cops had found their way up to his floor. He suspected it had something to do with the superior coffee. He didn't know the names of these officers. It was easier most times not to bother learning them because of the quick rate at which they disappeared. However, the upcoming election was a subject that greatly interested him.

"I think Ferguson would do a great job," said the other officer.

Nigel grabbed the edge of his desk, his knuckles whitening. He didn't want to interrupt their conversation, but found he couldn't stop himself. "Ferguson? You want four more years of the same bad decisions?"

The two cops turned to face him. The one who'd said Ferguson gave a half shrug. "I don't think the state's so bad."

Nigel wanted to hit him. He knew it was never a good idea to talk about politics. Especially with ignorant people, and that was how he viewed anyone who supported Ferguson. "J. Howard Edmondson is going to take great strides in making our state completely dry. You realize that means we'll have more work ahead of us? You realize that is job security for us?"

"Well, sir, I didn't think of it that way."

"You didn't think at all. A vote for Edmondson is a vote for Oklahoma." He'd read that on a sign on his way to work this morning and liked it.

"You don't think the Republican Party is a better choice?"

Nigel scoffed. "Oklahoma will always be a Democratic state." He lifted a finger to point at the young cop's face, a gesture both indignant and rude. "And don't you forget it."

He turned away from the conversation, away from his desk, and strode from the room, angry with himself, angry at everything.

Chapter 7

Robert

The truck didn't purr; it was more of a rumble that he could feel all around and deep within him. Robert's nerves shook his body that matched the rhythm of the truck. He couldn't believe he was doing this, but the thought of Rebecca Lewis stirred his rebellious nature just enough. Charles was right; it was time for a change.

He stopped the truck half a block down from Becky's place, the agreed on rendezvous point. He'd spoken to her just briefly on the phone, terror bringing his voice down to a low whisper. He wanted her to say yes, and he wanted her to say no. What she said was, "I'm surprised to hear you asking me this. Won't your daddy be mad?"

His words came out in that same hushed whisper and also surprised him. "Yeah, he will. But I don't care if it means I get to see you."

She had hummed a yes in his ear, a more resounding purr than the old work truck could hope to make. It was the single greatest sound Robert Arrington had heard in his life. He hoped to hear it many, many more times.

He didn't have to wait in the truck for long before he saw Becky leave her house and walk toward him. A slight Oklahoma breeze came rustling through the trees, catching her long blonde hair and the hem of her skirt.

Her hair danced with the wind and her skirt fluttered, revealing an ideal portion of her milky thighs, a sight that would haunt Robert the rest of his adolescence.

She climbed in the truck and smiled at him. "I can't believe we're actually doing this."

He smiled in return. "Neither can I. Where do your parents think you're going?"

"To the hayride and the Fall Festival, of course. What about your parents?"

"They're both at the Festival. I got grounded today for talking back to my dad. But Dad's hired hand, Charles, talked me into doing this."

"Seems I owe Charles my gratitude."

"You just may. What do you think we should do?"

She smiled again, but this time her smile brought with it a curious new side, something wild and exciting. He felt another flutter in his chest and a squirm in his gut, not a pleasant feeling, but one he enjoyed nonetheless.

"Ever been to Wewah Point?" she asked, her voice in a near whisper as if she was afraid to mention the popular make-out spot by name.

He smiled this time, not his normal carefree one, but a genuine one that convinced Becky she'd done the right thing in coming out with him. Fortunately, in the dark of the cab, she couldn't see the red that burned his cheeks. He said, "You know I haven't."

She closed the distance between them on the bench seat and placed a hand on his knee. A shock of excitement shot through him. She leaned into him and whispered right into his ear, "Then let's go." Prickles of gooseflesh broke out all along his neck.

He took the roads in town nice and slow but once he got the truck heading north on 281, he pushed down on the gas, his hand expertly moving the gearshift into place, throwing it from second to third and up to fourth, a gear this truck had not found in years. After switching to fourth gear, the hum of the motor turned to a roar and filled the cab, overriding any conversation the pair may have had. His hand came off the gear shift knob and, in a gesture too bold to even consider, landed on her exposed knee. She didn't remove it.

While the ride to Wewah Point carried with it no stimulating conversation, it did provide excitement and anticipation. They almost missed their turn, partly because of the extreme focus on each other, and partly because neither of them had been to the Point. There wasn't exactly a sign guiding would-be fornicators.

When they came to it, there was only one other car there. Steam covered the inside of the windows and the sight of it brought the realization home of what he was about to do. He'd heard of steamed windows, he understood the idea behind it, but never pictured himself to be the one on the inside, creating the steam.

"We're here." Despite the fact that Becky still spoke in a whisper, it sounded incredibly loud. With her face just inches from his, he didn't want to think about it a second longer. He pressed his lips to hers. With a passion unknown to anyone save teenagers and poets, the couple came together in that old work truck, experimenting with a thing more potent and more addictive than any form of alcohol.

A scattered thought entered Robert's head along the lines of, "Let them keep prohibition on, but never let them outlaw this."

Despite the passion and the desire between the two, they were both inexperienced and it became clear they were unsure of how far the other wanted to go. There was a timid effort on the part of Robert to fondle at the bottom of her blouse, but he quickly realized he was already out of his league with the kissing and adding her breasts into the mix wouldn't help at all.

Her hands roved over his body, finding his chest, his back, his neck, his face. Her touch electrified his skin, and that along with the intertwining of their tongues, brought his penis to full attention. It ached in his pants, a feeling not quite unpleasant, and not quite new. They tipped ever closer to the edge of a sin they'd never experienced, and one they couldn't forget once they had lost that innocence.

When her fingers brushed at the front of his jeans, she pulled away from him, panting hard, and locked her eyes on his. "Hi."

Also panting and unsure if he should laugh or be outraged at the end of what was so good, he responded, "Hello." He smiled. He couldn't quite stop his face from breaking out in the purest form of joy.

"How are you?"

"Quite good. How are you?"

"Very much the same. I thought we should maybe take a breather. What do you think?"

Every part of him wanted to say no, but he remembered that church would be in just two days and he could already imagine the guilt he would feel. Brother Ezekiel had a way of looking into his very soul and seeing anything he should be ashamed of. Three or four times he'd walked the lonely isle to the front during the altar call to admit to some sin or another. Ezekiel would pray over him and assure him that his sins were forgiven. After church his father would always ask why he'd gone to the front and always Robert felt compelled to tell. He saw it as a way of admitting his weaknesses and becoming stronger. At least, he used to. In the cab of the dirty work truck with the beauty beside him and the erection dying in his jeans, he wondered if it had made him stronger, if he had, in fact, gotten himself into trouble for no reason.

At last, with the images of Brother Ezekiel standing in the pulpit running through his mind, he nodded. "Yeah, a breather wouldn't be a bad thing. Are you going to church on Sunday?"

She laughed, a sound the angels in Heaven would be jealous of. "There's a way to kill the mood."

He laughed with her. "Sorry, I wanted to talk about something."

Next to them, in the darkness that surrounded them, the car with the steamed windows began to rock back and forth. Robert and Becky watched, a mixture of dread and joy crossing their faces. Both were willing to rebel but only to a point. Their fear kept them from the experiences they longed for but didn't understand.

"Want to drive around?" she asked after a moment of watching the car rocking.

"I do, but…"

"Yes?"

"Can we come back again some time?"

She giggled again, that same tinkling sound better than Heaven. "I would like that."

He started the truck, rolled down his window to let the steam from the inside roll out, and backed out of the parking spot.

Chapter 8

Ezekiel

The smell of popcorn and funnel cakes hung over the air like a warm blanket while bright lights flashed on and off from the various rides planted in the blocked off streets. Laughter of adults and children alike was the overwhelming soundtrack. Ezekiel spoke with his parishioners as he saw them. Frank Underhill and his wife Samantha watched their teenage daughter Gretchen try to win a prize at one of the booths. He stood by the proud parents and watched their daughter. She'd been born shortly before he'd come to town and it had been a difficult pregnancy, so they had settled for just the one. As they put it, they felt blessed to have been given a single miracle.

He stopped by the Ferris wheel, not a big one, but big enough for their small town. He watched it spin and waved at young Ed and his wife Irene. They snuggled up close together as the wheel spun them to the top. Their love for each other brought a smile to his tired face. He bought a large pretzel and dipped it in a small cup of cheese. He thought it funny that something so unhealthy was perfectly legal while alcohol was not. Other people hurried around him, their shouts and excitement brightening his evening. So much had been heavy recently that he'd needed something like this.

He saw Johnny's car pull back into the parking spot next to Holder Drug. He sauntered over, dropping his napkin and his cheese cup in the trashcan he passed on his way to the car. He shoved the last of the pretzel in his mouth then slid into the passenger seat of the car. "That was quick," he said.

Johnny, or Wild Johnny as he preferred to be called, said, "He's not budging, boss. We'll have to take some more extreme measures."

Ezekiel swallowed the pretzel. "Maybe we could drop him a little extra cash. Buy him out?"

Johnny lifted an eyebrow. "Going soft on me?"

Ezekiel sighed. "Were that I could. I just thought for a moment that maybe it would be that simple. Okay, Johnny, you know what to do."

Wild Johnny nodded. "Want him to keep one kneecap?"

"I suppose it depends on how he reacts to losing one. Hey, and take Charlie with you, will you? That kid wants to rise up and he seems promising."

"Sure thing, boss."

He stepped out of the car and went back across the street to the Festival. He reflected on the conversation while he wandered around the Square, watching the sights and hearing the sounds of the Fall Festival, which helped to alleviate the stress. The distinct aroma of booze hung on the air like the fall decorations, which meant more money in his pockets. There may have been some rough edges in his bootlegging operation with those foolish enough to attempt to make their own, but he still made more money than anyone in town. As long as he lined the pockets of those in charge, he could keep this up indefinitely. And as long as it remained illegal.

During his stroll he came across one of his least favorite people escorted by one of his favorites: Mike Arrington and his wife, Lucy. Mike wore his typical denim overalls that were unflattering but, Ezekiel supposed, functional. Lucy wore a dress that revealed enough of her legs to satisfy most of the patrons of the Festival. Ezekiel smiled at them both and shook Mike's hand.

"How are we this fine evening?" he asked.

"Not too bad," Mike replied. He carried a cup of water. Ezekiel was sure that was all the man ever drank. And when he got upset about prohibition ending, he wasn't kidding around. The man really loathed anything that might change the temperament of the one partaking.

"Lucy." Ezekiel dipped his head to the deacon's wife.

"Preacher," she responded.

"I had to take a break from the truck to get a drink." Mike indicated the cup he carried. "It's hot work pulling the hay all around the Square, but the kids love it."

Ezekiel lifted an eyebrow. "Oh? But I thought young Robert would be pulling the truck this evening."

"Yes," he coughed, "the boy still doesn't know his place at times. It is the curse of the teenager, I believe, to go against the will of their parents. I had to take over to show him I mean what I say when I say it."

Lucy said nothing but stood a step behind her husband and kept her eyes on Ezekiel. He tried to ignore her, but found his own eyes drifting in her direction several times.

He patted Mike's shoulder. "A parent knows what is best for their children. I believe he was looking forward to this night. Maybe that will solidify some of your authority over him."

"I know he wanted to be here. He wanted to see some girl." He shrugged. "Another time for that." Despite the hard edge he took when speaking about his son's discipline, Ezekiel thought he could hear some real regret in Mike's voice. "Well, back to the truck." He downed the rest of his water and walked away from his wife and preacher without a backward glance.

Ezekiel's eyes locked on Lucy, a sight much preferred to that of Mike in his overalls. "He's too hard on the boy," Ezekiel said, a smile tugging at his mouth. He thought of running his hands through her blond hair, her full lips pressed against his own, their tongues fighting for purchase in each other's mouths. They began to walk together, her body feeling like the sun next to him, a constant presence weighing on his mind.

She nodded and brushed a hand through her hair. She'd curled it for the evening and pulled part of it back, revealing the tips of her round, petite ears. "If I try to intervene on Robert's behalf, he yells at me instead. He's quite the Godly man."

"Let's not speak ill of those who are not in attendance."

"Oh, Ezekiel, you can drop the act. There's no one else around."

He glanced and realized they'd managed to find themselves in a secluded part of the Square, nearly hidden in shadows cast by the lights of the festivities. "In that case, I hate that fucker."

She laughed, a sound that stood out from the other joyous sounds at the festival like diamond among rocks. Mike never noticed what a treasure he had.

Mike and Lucy had gone to high school together and

the four-year difference in their ages didn't matter to the young and impressionable Lucy Taylor who saw dating a senior as a badge of honor, and despite the fact that he was a goody-two-shoes, her friends still envied her when they cruised the Boulevard on Friday nights. It made her feel remarkable. And somewhere along the way, she foolishly fell in love and stayed with him. They married her junior year and Robert was born the next year. She didn't graduate high school.

"Well," she said, "it seems my husband is busy for the next couple of hours. Wanna go somewhere and pray?"

Ezekiel felt a stirring in his groin that he so wanted to take advantage of. He glanced around once more. "Not now." He shook his head. "Not that I don't want to. I have a meeting soon."

She smiled and brushed a hand across the front of his pants. "It won't take long."

The stirring in his groin turned into a growling and he grabbed her hand. "Careful, or I might have to take you up on that."

She leaned in close to his ear and panted, "That's what I'm hoping for."

His house, the church parsonage, stood only a couple blocks from the Square, so it took them less than two minutes to walk the distance. They slipped through the shadows and went unnoticed by most at the Festival. Those who did notice didn't care.

The affair had been going on for the better part of ten years and Ezekiel had enjoyed nearly every moment of it, even those times they'd nearly been caught, as it seemed all adulterers must do from time to time. He wasn't sure he could ever love another woman, but his caring for Lucy Arrington went far beyond what he would consider mere love.

Obviously the head deacon's wife leaving her husband for the preacher would be scandalous in the small town and would mean the end of the preacher's career, both of them. So they kept their affair secret, meeting when and where they could.

So Lucy knew little about him, except what he liked in bed, while he knew a great deal about her. But it was all right by them; they got to have sex and not worry about the complications of a relationship.

After they finished their rendezvous for the evening, Lucy attempted to get her hair back to its glory, while Ezekiel tugged on his pants and tucked his shirt back in. He felt a little envious of the dress that Lucy didn't have to remove; she'd just climbed on and enjoyed the ride.

They strolled back to the Square but separated before they got to the edge of the festivities. "Here is where I leave you," he said, just as the Ferris wheel came into view again.

"Just for tonight, I hope."

"Only for tonight," he agreed, offering her hand a quick squeeze before slipping away from her.

He saw Johnny's car park in the same spot. He meandered over and plopped in, his body a relaxed ball after the cheerful orgasm.

"Well?" he asked.

Johnny lit a cigarette, the flash from the light momentarily lighting up his face. "He's in pain, but he still isn't giving in. You may have to visit him."

Ezekiel waved a hand. The anger he'd felt earlier now subsided. "It can wait. Give him a little more time."

"Boss? You all right?"

Visions of Lucy Arrington pulling her panties back up under her dress ran though his mind. “Indeed I am. I’ve got to get my sermon prepared. See you in church?”

“Ha!”

Ezekiel walked away from Johnny’s car. He knew he would have to do something about Hank, but for the moment, he could sell his booze and think that was okay. Ezekiel Wilson would pay him a visit, and when Ezekiel visited people on official business, there could be no witnesses.

****

Arriving in a small town, freshly married, as the First Baptist Church’s new preacher, life simply could not have been better for Ezekiel Wilson. He got what he wanted out of marriage: making love, prayer, Bible study, and constant companionship. Mary spoke often of the charm of small town life. She was the perfect pastor’s wife. She began hosting a ladies’ tea on Sunday afternoons at the parsonage, the house owned by the church where the preacher lived. Ezekiel would spend those afternoons in his basement study, preparing the sermon for the Sunday evening church and for the youth class he taught on Wednesdays. Everything was perfect.

Until it wasn’t.

The first cracks began to appear in the facade just a few months after Mary and Ezekiel moved to town. Not in their marriage, but in the dream. Ezekiel had always believed, since he’d become a Believer, that God had called him to be a preacher, a “fisher of men” as it were, and yet this church that he’d been called to seemed to be on the very edge of closure. The previous preacher could not make sense of budgets, so he’d convinced the church, or at least one of the many committees, to hire his wife as the treasurer, but she was worse with finances than he was. They got off before the ship could sink, and now Ezekiel found himself needing to perform miracles akin to, if not Jesus, then at least the Apostles.

Mary stayed by his side encouraging all avenues of giving that they could. He preached moving sermons on the importance of tithes and offerings. The deacons put a stop to that, informing him that their members sought sermons on sin and not on giving.

On a Thursday afternoon, Ezekiel took off from the church early and spent the hours in bed with his wife. The sheets stuck to their sweaty skin. Mary's head rose and fell on Ezekiel's chest. As he drifted in the post-orgasm delight of the day, Mary spoke to him.

"I have an idea," she said. Ezekiel opened his eyes and gazed down at the black hair of his wife.

Her glorious hair tickled his naked skin. His fingers twitched in their desire to scratch at it. He always got a little squirmy before falling asleep.

"Remember my uncle who makes moonshine?" she said, her face still turned away from him.

He smiled at the mention of the uncle. He always enjoyed a man who did not care for modern day beliefs and did what he wanted. He held no worries about the laws that prohibited alcohol sales and took it upon himself to make it and sell it.

She said, "He told me, the last time that we saw him, that he made a great deal of money from selling his moonshine."

She lifted her head, her blue eyes meeting his brown ones. "He said it's not that hard to make."

Ezekiel listened the way a husband might listen with a football game on in the background. Her words impacted him the way a light snow would caress the skin.

"Do you think we should try it?" she asked.

"Try what?" he asked, lost in her eyes, in her voice, in the moment.

She turned from him again, not returning to rest her head on his chest, but facing the window. Ezekiel could make out her profile, the afternoon sun smoothing away the worry lines she'd recently developed.

She said, "I think we should. Not all laws are worth obeying."

Breaking laws seemed like something Ezekiel would want to avoid, but his wife looked so pretty, and he didn't want to upset her. "So you want…" He trailed off, hoping she would continue the thought.

"To make and sell moonshine. If we can, maybe more. Kansas isn't too far and if they end prohibition then we could buy there and sell here."

As she spoke, each word pounded a new hope in Ezekiel's mind. He'd all but decided to pack up and leave this church, hoping to find something more stable somewhere else. But here was an answer. Could it work? he wondered.

"We'll need a few things," Mary continued, the sheet slipped from her, exposing her milky-white breast with the pink jellybean nipple on the end of it. Ezekiel stared, not daring to believe his luck of being able to behold such a sight. "I'll call my uncle." She turned and found him staring and smiled at him. "We'll have time for more of that later. We've got work to do."

Once Mary had the idea, it didn't take long for her to drive it forward. Ezekiel hung on tight as they careened around every obstacle in their way. Money started coming in shortly after the making of the moonshine, and they funneled it into the church. Nearly every dime. They kept some for supplies and the occasional night out.

In the beginning, they had to find people they could trust to sell the product for them. Mostly, they used alcoholics and paid them in booze. Obviously, the Baptist preacher couldn't go around selling alcohol, no matter what the money might go toward. The only thing worse would be if someone caught him dancing.

Ezekiel would often reflect later that if he'd known where this would all lead, he would have simply packed up and moved on, but he couldn't know. The decisions his wife made that afternoon in bed would change the trajectory of his whole life.

Chapter 9

Nigel

That first Tuesday night of November, Nigel awaited the news with silent trepidation. He'd made at least three bets with some of the beat cops in his division, and he didn't want to appear foolish to them. He knew his state, and he was sure that the law would not be revoked, not yet.

The polls officially closed an hour earlier. It would take some time to roll through each of the ballots, but he believed it wouldn't take that long to determine that they would still have prohibition in the morning.

He pulled his pocket watch from his inner pocket one more time. Three minutes had passed since he'd last checked it. He replaced it and pulled a tiny comb from another inner pocket of his suit and proceeded to comb his insubstantial mustache with it. Combing it did little more than give him something to do with his hands.

Another sip of coffee and another tick of the clock. Nigel would be trapped here if prohibition did fail. He had plans to rise up, but his plans included enforcing the dry laws of the land. By the end of the night, the great state of Oklahoma would have a new governor, and this could be Nigel's chance.

He sighed. He leaned over his desk, placed the coffee cup beside his neat rows of pencils and stared down at the map of Oklahoma. He had that northwest area circled. It was the place, given the opportunity, where he would go.

Minutes passed and Nigel, unable to take the quiet anymore, stood to go home. Before he could take a step, a young officer, one of those who'd placed a bet with Nigel, walked up to his desk.

"Yes?" Nigel said.

Wordlessly, the officer handed over a hundred-dollar bill. Nigel accepted the money with a smile. "Thank you, Officer."

The young man shook his head and stalked off. Nigel felt a triumph roll through him that had little to do with the bill clutched in his hand.

Chapter 10

Robert

With Thanksgiving rapidly approaching, the farm moved with the preparations of the holiday. They'd already sold two dozen of their three dozen turkeys, and those would have to be slaughtered and plucked in the coming days.

Robert loathed this holiday.

He enjoyed his family and the time he got to spend with them on the actual holiday, but the days leading up to and the days following it were among his least favorite of the year. And this year, it was even more unbearable knowing that with his schedule packed as tightly as it was, he would have less and less time to spend with Becky.

In the weeks since their first trip to Wewah Point, the couple had managed only one other excursion to the popular make-out place. His parents still knew nothing about his rebelliousness, but he was sure he wouldn't be able to hide it forever. He had voiced this to Becky who would nonchalantly shut him down. She didn't want to talk about the future. She only wanted to focus on "the now" as she called it. In church, they were often told to live each day as if it was the last, and Becky held that mantra in her heart, though probably not in the way the preacher meant it.

Since he'd stolen the truck for the night and lied to his parents, Robert had to confide in someone and the only likely candidate was the young Australian farmhand. Charlie didn't put a lot of stock in the idea of God, the whole notion of religion being sort of silly to him, so he had a lot more faith in man's ability to further his life without a god.

That Saturday before Thanksgiving, Charlie led the turkeys to Robert in the barn. Together the two would grab the turkeys by legs that felt like spindly sticks that ended in thorns. They would lodge the turkey's head down in a shoot with just enough neck exposed to cut it. Robert handled the knife deftly as he had for the four previous Thanksgivings since he decided he could handle the slaughtering on his own. After removing the head, they would let the blood drain from the bird. While the blood pooled in the bucket under the turkey, Charlie would talk, telling stories of his own adventures in Australia.

Robert listened with as much patience as he could, but he had to tell Charlie about Becky.

After the blood drained, they would dip the turkey into boiling water which would help the feathers come off easier, then with the turkey hanging from a hook, they would pluck. Robert finally found his chance to talk. "Hey, remember the Fall Festival?"

"Sure. The night you skipped out and stole your father's truck?"

Robert's cheeks burned. "That's the night, yeah. Well, things have gone pretty well with Becky."

At the mention of her name, Robert's face broke out into a huge smile. The hired hand turned and threw a handful of feathers at him. "Right. You've got to give me a bit more, mate."

"Mate? Five years I've known you and you've never called me 'mate.' "

"Sorry, at times I slip back into the accent. Now tell me."

Robert laughed and wiped the feathers from his face and shoulders. "The only thing I can really say is, you were right. Taking the old man's truck that night was brilliant. Now I just need a way to see her again. We've been too busy lately. I've got to get out."

"See who again?" The voice, booming and full of menace, filled the barn and shot ice water through Robert's veins. He turned around to see his father standing not ten feet from them. They'd been so preoccupied with plucking they hadn't noticed when Mike walked into the barn. "Who is it you're talking about, son?"

"Dad, I…it's no one, I just was goofing around with Charlie."

"Goofing around? Did I hear you say you took my truck one night to see someone?"

Robert glanced at Charlie but he no longer found a friend in the Australian. Instead he saw someone who thought that plucking every last feather from a turkey's butt was the most fascinating thing ever.

"Dad, come on, Charlie and I are just talking. We have to do something while we're doing this." It was all he could do to think quickly and not turn and run.

Charlie began to say something, but Mike cut him off with a wave of the hand. "Go outside, Charlie. I'll deal with you in a moment. Right now, I'm talking to my son."

The hired hand, always dutiful, peeled off his

gloves, leaving them and the feathers on the floor. Robert didn't watch him go, but stood waiting for the storm that would soon be unleashed on him.

"Now you're going to tell me the truth, boy. Who were you talking about?"

"Dad, you have to…" But what Mike had to do was cut off by a backhand across the mouth.

"That sounded like you were going to lie to me. Now tell me *the truth*." The last two words came out in a whisper that was so menacing, it made the hair on the back of Robert's neck stand up. He had ventured into unwanted territory, into a place he'd never thought to come.

Still something in him, probably the very part of him that prevented his hand from rubbing his face after that backhand to the face, held firm to the lie he wanted to tell. "I'm not lying to you, Dad, I don't want to seem like a square to Charlie, so I tell him stuff sometimes. I'm sorry."

Mike raised his arm again, ready to backhand his son one more time but held when Robert's eyes did not drop from his own. Robert watched him wrestle with the internal anger that wanted to crash out into the world. "I oughta hit you again just for lying to that poor boy. You know what? I think I will. Turn around and grab the table."

"What? No, Dad, that's not necessary."

"I'll decide what's necessary, now grab the table." He pulled his belt from the belt loops. Robert saw this and also saw no way out. This was the least he deserved, he decided, and better than he would have gotten had his father gotten the truth out of him. He grabbed the table.

The first time the belt flew across his backside, he

cried out; he couldn't help it. The belt sent pain right up through him in a way the backhand hadn't. After ten, he couldn't feel them anymore. He knew the damage that could be done by his father's leather belt so he didn't attempt to fool himself into believing he wouldn't be feeling the pain later.

With each swing of the belt, he softened the blows by picturing Becky and her sweet, addictive smile. Somewhere in the darkest part of his mind, where he kept his secret desires and his sins, he felt something come loose and slip to the front of his mind. It was the hem of Becky's dress from the night at Wewah Point; right there at his fingertips, he could see the milky white of her thighs, could nearly feel the heat from those legs, and in his mind, he didn't let the hem stop his hand, but thrust it right passed, to the point of no return, to the heat and moisture held secret between her legs.

Even if he couldn't sit down tomorrow, he would carry this thought with him. It would bloom until it became more than simple teenage desire; it would become action. He would taste her flesh and she would taste his, and damn his soul for thinking it, but there was no way he would be telling the preacher about it the next Sunday.

His father quit at twenty licks and luckily for Robert the old man could not see his face, because the smile there would have set him off again.

Chapter 11

Ezekiel

On the following Sunday morning, Ezekiel sat behind his desk preparing the words he no longer believed. The Bible lay opened before him, the pages marked and highlighted from years of use. He closed his eyes, feigning prayer, and thought of his first love, a girl named Mary.

He pictured the contrast of her pale colored skin and black hair that stirred the primal instincts of his soul from the first moment he saw her. In high school, he'd known girls, girls he had thought were beautiful and sensuous, but Mary changed all that. She put beauty into perspective so that he no longer had to wonder just what it was.

He had first seen her during his freshman year of college at the state's Baptist University. He'd gone to explore the avenues God wanted him to go down. She'd gone for the same thing. He hoped to one day lead a flock, she hoped to one day be a preacher's wife. No doubt she was a perfect match for him, so he set about talking to her in any and every way he could.

From those first few days, the two began to fall in love with each other, because while he was noticing her, she was noticing him. He'd never planned for it. He went to college to fulfill God's will in his life. He did not suspect that he might meet someone so life-changing in the flesh.

They studied the Bible together, prayed together, but very rarely did they have physical contact. So the rare treat of kissing became legendary in the mind of young Ezekiel.

Sitting at his desk, he remembered the first time they'd kissed, sitting in his car, with moonlight and streetlights streaming in through the windows, casting more shadows than illumination. The moment felt right, so while Mary spoke, Ezekiel leaned over, took her face in his hand, and pressed his lips to hers. She held back for a moment, surprised by the timing of it, but then she returned the kiss, opening her mouth to allow his tongue to find hers. The kiss lasted only a short time before she pulled away and smiled at him. It was that smile he would always remember, that would always bring out his own smile, the only joyful smile he would have again. And thinking of it now, he felt the edges of his mouth tug up in the infrequent expression.

That's how Mike found Ezekiel: sitting behind his desk, the Bible opened in front of him, with a sweet smile on his face.

"Sorry to bother you, Brother Ezekiel, but I had hoped to catch you before church and speak with you about something."

Ezekiel had a difficult time not picking up the Bible in front of him and hurling it at Mike's head. Being pulled out of such a pleasant memory was not something he enjoyed, especially for something as trivial as another one of Mike's problems. He seemed to not be able to make decisions without first consulting the preacher. When his wife wanted to have another child shortly after

Ezekiel had come to town, he'd spent hours with the preacher. Since then, Mike had decided to run a great number of things by Brother Ezekiel, and the preacher always answered in a way he knew Mike would want to hear.

"Not a problem, Mike, come on in. You caught me praying. I've got a good message this morning."

"Staying with the twenty-third chapter of Proverbs?"

"It's done well so far, hasn't it?"

"Sure, sure. I was wondering if I could talk to you about my boy, about Robert?"

"Why of course, Mike, come on and sit down." He looked at his watch. "We've got about ten minutes if you can handle that."

Mike sat. "Thank you, sir."

"Now, what have I told you about calling me 'sir'?"

"Right, I'm sorry."

"You do seem agitated. What's going on with Robert?"

"I walked in last night on him talking with Charles, my hired hand. What he said bothered me, but he told me he was making up the stories to impress Charles. Now, I punished him for lying, but I'm starting to think he was lying to me, not Charles."

"I see. And what makes you think Robert would start doing that?"

"He mentioned something about taking my truck. I wouldn't think anything about it, but I keep strict records for the fuel in the work truck. I just like to make sure that nothing's going wrong with my trucks."

Ezekiel nodded, though he was sure that's not what Mike was doing. Likely he strictly kept track of the fuel to ensure no one was stealing from him. Mike was a good man, but God forgive him if he ever caught someone stealing from him; he'd likely be convicted of murder, a thought Ezekiel kept in the back of his mind every time he visited Mike's wife.

"Anyway, I have a quarter tank of gas unaccounted for some time around the Fall Festival. And again a couple weeks later."

This piqued Ezekiel's interest, though he carefully hid that interest. "You don't think he took the truck without your permission?"

Mike sighed. "I would never have believed it, but you should have heard the way he was talking to Charles. He did mention a girl, and I have noticed that he's spending a lot more time on the phone and daydreaming lately. This is our busy time of year with the turkeys and the Christmas trees, so I need him to be all in. I've been trying to observe his behavior a little closer."

"That does make sense." Ezekiel glanced at his watch again and made a decision. "I'll talk to him." He held up a hand to cut off Mike's objections. "I won't mention anything we talked about here, but I will try to get him to confide in me. The most important thing for him is to ask for forgiveness for these sins. If it turns out that your suspicions are groundless, I will tell you and let your mind rest."

Ezekiel stood and grabbed up his big and well-used Bible while Mike thanked him endlessly. Ezekiel didn't have time to listen to this man's madness for hours. He would talk to the boy and he would do it today, but first, he had to make sure his flock heard his words.

The pulpit in the church was a wooden cross with a place on his side to rest his overly large Bible. After a prayer, he stood behind the cross, his hands resting on the recently varnished wood. He waited a beat before breaking into the sermon.

"Good people, there is not a better place to be on God's green Earth on this day than in His house!" That got a roaring approval from the crowd: at least three people said, "Amen."

"As we near the holiday of giving thanks, we are reminded of all the things that we must give thanks for: The Sun! The Sky! The Very Air We Breathe!" Each word received as much importance as any.

"However, even as we celebrate and give thanks, we are still being persecuted. How many of you all know someone who has been challenged by the *drink*?"

He paused for a moment to gaze at his audience. Several raised their hands amid the near-packed audience. He stole a glance at Lucy sitting dutifully by her husband on the front row. "Not everyone has raised their hand, which is a good sign, but with prohibition going, isn't even one hand too many?" Another chorus of "Amen" echoed the sanctuary. "Yes, of course it is. Now you good people came together just two weeks ago and managed to vote for the continuation of prohibition, which is a good sign. But this new Democrat, a 'wet,' whom we elected, seems to be determined to change that. We cannot allow him to take away one of the things that makes this state what it is today.

"I know there are illegal drinks, just as I know there are lots of other illegal activities in this town. It pains me to say it, oh yes, it does, but what point is there in hiding from the truth. If we want to clean it up, we can, but we'll have to be determined and we'll have to *want* it."

On the word "want," he slammed his fist into the

podium, causing a loud boom that reverberated around the room. He saw a few of the younger people jump, including Robert Arrington. He'd spotted the boy sitting with the rest of the youth group and kept swinging his gaze over to him.

He continued. "Governor Edmondson wants to bring about destruction to our state, our land, the place we call home and would continue to call home. 'We know we belong to the land, and the land we belong to is grand,' right? We cannot, should not, allow that to stop being true. As Christians we must confirm our place in Heaven and to do that, we must oppose anyone who seeks to bring the Devil into our land."

He carried on that way for nearly an hour. At the end of the sermon, during the altar call, nineteen people came to the front, some to kneel before the cross and pray, and others to come to him and confess their transgressions. Several were his customers, but he didn't worry about that. Every one of them had confessed and recommitted their spoiled lives at one point or another, and all had gone back to the bottle, a bottle he gave like a mother to a newborn baby.

Robert, Ezekiel noticed, did not come forward, but sat stone-faced, two rows behind his father. He did not appear to have the smallest bit of guilt behind those eyes. Ezekiel could see the beginnings of a change in the young man. He liked what he saw.

When Robert came through the line to shake hands with the preacher as everyone left the Lord's house for the week, Ezekiel grabbed him and pulled him to the side.

"I spoke with your father this morning."

The boy, just shy of eighteen, would not meet his

eyes. “Yes, sir,” he mumbled.

“Now I need you to come by the parsonage this afternoon. I would like to speak with you further.”

Robert’s eyes flashed up for just an instant and Ezekiel saw anger welling up in them. “Yes, sir.”

In those two words, Ezekiel was sure he discerned the boy’s intention of not coming. So Ezekiel grabbed the boy’s arm and squeezed, making it hurt just enough to get his attention. “It would not be wise to ignore my request. Just because you’re coming to talk with me does not mean I will be telling Mike everything we talk about.”

Robert lifted his head and stared into Ezekiel’s eyes. He must have seen something in them because he said, “Okay. I will be there.”

Ezekiel released his arm and went back to the line. He didn’t doubt the boy’s sincerity, knowing he would show. And Ezekiel would plant seeds in him and maybe, he could get himself a new employee down the line. He wondered briefly if Lucy would object to that.

Chapter 12

Robert

When the afternoon rolled around, Robert stood on the front porch of the parsonage. He had lifted his hand three times to ring the bell, but each time had let it fall. Something sinister inside him squirmed. He didn't want to be here, he didn't want to have to confess that he had lied to his dad and had been making out with Becky. He didn't want to have to say that he'd learned how to masturbate and found great pleasure thinking about the hem of Becky's skirt while he did it.

But he was here and saw no way around it. He lifted his hand a fourth time but this time, rang the bell. He heard it buzz on the other side of the door and a few moments later, Brother Ezekiel opened it, wearing jeans and a button-up shirt. It was the most dressed down Robert had ever seen the pastor. He didn't even know the man owned jeans.

"Ah, Robert, come in, come in." He held the door open and Robert entered. Personally, Robert had never been in the parsonage and found it much more appealing than he thought he would. He had to remind himself that Ezekiel had only been married a short time, so this was the house of a bachelor. He had no woman like Robert's mother around attempting to bring some femininity to it.

"I trust you found the place just fine," Ezekiel said

once they'd settled in the living room. Robert sat in a chair opposite Ezekiel's own chair and started to answer when the preacher interrupted him. "I'm only kidding," he said with a hearty chuckle.

Robert laughed. He was sure this was a different man than the fire and brimstone version he saw in the pulpit each Sunday. Despite the slight tremor in his hands, he relaxed.

"I suppose you can guess why I asked you to come by here today." His demeanor still held some of the humor, so Robert didn't tense up at the statement.

"You mentioned…" Robert cleared the gunk out of his throat. "You mentioned that you spoke with my dad."

"And do you know why he came to me?"

"Er…no, sir."

"Don't you?" He paused, giving Robert a chance to say something. When he didn't, Ezekiel continued, "It seems he has some growing concerns over your recent behaviors. I told him I wouldn't say exactly what we spoke of, but I will say that he thinks you've been lying to him."

Robert's gaze abruptly fell to the floor, the tremor that had been dissipating from his hands returned with ferocity.

"Again," Ezekiel continued, "I am accusing you of nothing, but I do want you to know that you have my confidence. I will spill nothing that happens in this house to your father. If he asks I will simply tell him that I am counseling. We must go forward trusting each other, and I want to promise you that."

Robert's hands stopped fidgeting; he leaned forward and stared intently at the preacher. "You really mean that?"

Ezekiel smiled. "Would you like me to swear on the Bible? Of course I mean it."

Robert's face broke into his own smile. "I'm glad to hear that, sir. I just had a feeling I wouldn't be able to say anything. If you were going to go straight to my dad and tell him everything, then I would suspect that we might as well just call him and invite him over here."

"Now you've got the right idea. Would you like a glass of tea?"

"Sure. Well," he wrinkled his nose, "it's not sweet, is it?"

"In this part of the state? Not even close."

The preacher jumped up and went into the next room. Robert could hear him opening the fridge and humming "Amazing Grace" as he worked. It was the song they'd sang during altar call that morning and Robert also had it stuck in his head. He took the chance to really absorb the room, noticing the sparse amount of decorations Ezekiel had. Near the chair the preacher had been using, Robert saw a small silver picture frame. Curious, he walked over and picked it up off the table.

It was a young woman, not much older than Robert, with dark hair that curled around her face. Though the picture was black and white, he could imagine the colors: lips of a delicate rose, eyes as dark as her hair, softly pale skin. The silver frame held a blackened tarnish from frequent handling.

Robert held on to the picture just a moment too long. "What have you got there?" Ezekiel entered the room, a glass of iced tea in each hand, the cubes clinking against the sides. He smiled.

Robert quickly turned to put the picture frame back where he got it. "I'm sorry," he stammered as he stumbled away from the chair.

The preacher stood still as stone, eyes darting from Robert to the picture frame. Once Robert was back in his seat, Ezekiel handed him his tea and returned to his own chair. He took a deep drink from his own glass before setting it on the table next to the picture frame.

"So you've met Mary."

Robert's cheeks burned, and the ice cubes danced within the glass to the rhythm of his shaking hand. "Sir?"

Ezekiel tenderly lifted the frame from the table. "This is Mary. Mary Morris. Well, Wilson. She was my wife."

Robert looked from the picture frame back to the preacher and back to the frame again in a mirror image of the way the preacher had looked at the two of them just a minute earlier. "Sir, I'm sorry. I shouldn't have looked."

"Of course you should have. What's the point of a picture if not for other people to look at it? If I didn't want you to see it, I would have put it away."

He never took his eyes off her. It was almost as if Robert wasn't in the room while Ezekiel held the picture.

Robert took a chance. "What happened, sir?" It was a legend among the other youth group kids that Ezekiel had been married once and something had happened to his wife. But the stories were outlandish, everything from her running off to being murdered in a mob hit.

"She was the loveliest girl in all of existence. I would've spent my life with her, trying all that I could to live up to her goodness." He sighed and put the frame back on the table. "She died after just two years of marriage."

"Died?" He swallowed. "I'm sorry to hear that."

"Not as sorry as I was."

"How did it happen?"

Ezekiel waved a hand at him. "Let's not go into that right now." He took another sip of tea and smacked his lips. "Let's focus on Rebecca Lewis."

Robert felt like the walls of the parsonage had all just collapsed on him. Every square inch of his lungs deflated and his heart burst into a speed that could have won the Kentucky Derby. "Er…Rebecca er…Lewis?" he managed to get out.

"Now, Bobby, can I call you Bobby?"

"Well, I, uh…"

"Good. Now, Bobby, you told me you would be straight with me, so don't sit there and pretend you weren't out with the Lewis girl while everyone else was at the Fall Festival."

Robert bent his head and let the tears that stung the corners of his eyes fall free. If he had to cry, he might as well do it now, he decided. Maybe the preacher would go a little easier on him. "How did you know?" he whispered.

"Well, I didn't. I merely suspected. I just thought I'd cast the net and see what I caught, just as Peter had done at Jesus' behest."

Robert lifted his head. "You didn't know? So my dad doesn't know?"

Ezekiel shrugged. "He suspects as well, but now I *do* know. So let's talk about her."

Robert wiped the tears off his face. "What do you want to know?"

"Have you…taken her innocence?"

Robert furiously shook his head.

"Well, then, what are you worrying about? I must

admit when I learned about the lying and put that together with the missing girl at the Festival, I really thought that must be what the two of you had done." He leaned back and crossed his legs. "I'm relieved."

Robert could feel the loosening of the ropes that had grown so tight over his chest. The airflow became less restricted and he could relax again. "You are really determined to cause me a heart attack, aren't you?"

The preacher laughed, a raucous sound that shook the house. "You got me on that, Bobby. You really got me." He drained the last of his tea.

The silence settled over them, and the two relaxed into it, both feeling comfortable. At last Robert cleared his throat and said, "The truth is, I snuck out without permission and picked up Becky. We made out a little, but that's all. That was the night of the Fall Festival, and we've only snuck out one more time since then."

The preacher nodded and smiled. He leaned forward. "Bobby, you've done nothing wrong."

That brought Robert's head up. He took a deep breath, staring at the preaching, attempting to understand what he meant. Words bounced around the inside of his head like a scratched record beating the same line over and over: *I lied. Kissed a girl. I lied. Kissed a girl.*

"I mean it, Bobby. So you lied. So you kissed a girl. So you lied again," Ezekiel said, as if hearing those repeating words. "You've simply done what all teenagers do. You know when I was your age I did those same things. I see your struggle with this, but I want you to understand, you are in control of your own life. You only have a year left under the roof of your father, and what then? Do you want to look back on this part of your life with regret?"

The glass Robert held slipped from his hand, but he didn't notice. "You can't be serious."

"Oh I am." Ezekiel stared down at the fallen glass, the ice cubes spilling out onto the carpet. "You wanna clean that up?"

"Huh?" Robert saw the glass and jumped to start picking it up. "I am so sorry!"

"It's quite all right. This isn't my house, technically speaking."

Once Robert had cleared the mess and was back to his chair, Ezekiel checked his watch. "I would wager we've uncovered a lot of the truth here and you probably feel like a load has been lifted." Robert nodded. "Then let's plan on meeting again next week to talk things over. Just remember to tell your father that you told me everything and that you'll change your ways. If you're careful you can keep up the façade without worry."

Robert smiled and stood. His whole body felt lighter and he had the notion to go find Becky now to see if her lips tasted different on Sunday afternoons.

Chapter 13

Ezekiel

The next several weeks saw a surge in sales for illegal alcohol; the holidays always boosted liquor sales. The five moonshiners whose booze went directly to Ezekiel couldn't keep up with the demand. Ezekiel had been forced to send crews to Kansas and Texas on multiple excursions to provide the booze they needed to make sales. It was so busy, Ezekiel forgot to worry about Hank Thomas, the moonshiner silly enough to not work under the preacher.

Wild Johnny had gone back three times, busted him around a little, burned down his barn, but still the man would not relent. He rebuilt and promised he would not give in to fear. Hank even attempted to call the cops, not realizing how deep Ezekiel lined their pockets. And the last time Johnny checked in on him, he'd acquired a crew of his own to help with the production of the moonshine. He even had Billy West working for him.

Now Wild Johnny stayed back in the shadows and observed. Killing Hank might be a necessary step, but Ezekiel wanted to proceed without shedding blood if at all possible.

The reason for the surge in sales was the rumor of prohibition ending. Ezekiel didn't put stock in rumors, but he fanned this one to help with his sales. He was enjoying more money than he had in his entire life. However, Inauguration Day was rapidly approaching and the new governor, J. Howard Edmondson, promised to end prohibition in Oklahoma once and for all. Ezekiel didn't see how that could possibly happen, but he'd seen stranger things in his life.

In the basement of the parsonage, Ezekiel could be himself. There was no danger of anyone coming down and finding him counting large stacks of bills. Sure, in theory, the members of the church could come in at any time as they were the technical owners of the house, but he knew that none would. And even if they did, they could never get in the basement without him opening the door for them.

"Boss?" Wild Johnny stood in the doorway, interrupting Ezekiel from his counting. Ezekiel paused. "I think we're going to have to do something about Hank Thomas." Johnny had been here waiting to say something to Ezekiel about the other moonshiner. Ezekiel let him wait; there was no reason to be bothered about anything with money in front of you. Apparently, Johnny's patience had run out.

"Hank Thomas? I thought you had him squared away? What's the problem, Johnny?"

"We may need to do something a little more serious. He's remaining defiant. There's a rumor that he's been selling to Edward." That got Ezekiel's attention; Edward was one of his biggest clients. "Plus he has Billy West working for him now. Billy keeps talking about the night you came to his house. You scared him and he feels Hank can protect him. This could hurt your reputation. Both of them."

Ezekiel slammed down the bills in his hand. A few

went flying. "That little bastard Billy still comes to my church every week. He sits in one of the pews and eats my bread and drinks my juice, and he has the audacity to work for the enemy and spread rumors about me?"

Wild Johnny took a step back from the preacher, clearly being familiar with Ezekiel's anger. Ezekiel watched as Johnny pulled a small bottle from his hip pocket and uncorked it. The scent perked every hair in Ezekiel's nostrils. He held out a hand for the bottle without waiting for Johnny to hand it to him. He threw his head back and poured. The clear liquid was nearly straight alcohol, and any mortal man might have passed out from the amount that Ezekiel downed. But Ezekiel Wilson was no mere mortal man.

He coughed and glanced down at the bottle. "Where'd you get that?"

"I got it from Hank."

Ezekiel, in the midst of wiping his mouth, paused and stared down at the bottle, tilting it back and forth in the light. "Hank made this?" He rolled the bottle from one hand to the other. "What'd it cost you?"

"He gave me a sample after I broke his arm."

He nodded as if he expected as much. "No wonder he doesn't want to work for me. He's probably making quite a lot of money himself with this."

Wild Johnny nodded. "Our booze is selling out, but his is priced much higher and he only caters to the upper-ended clients. I've seen them come and go from his place. It's no secret that he makes it. He's paying off the cops and the right people, perhaps better than you are."

Ezekiel stood and held the bottle up to the light. It could have been water. "This is a remarkable thing."

He reared back his arm and smashed the bottle into

the wall. The glass crunched and bits sliced his hand. Blood snaked its way down his arm into his white, long-sleeved shirt. He stared down at the blood on his hand and smiled. It made him feel alive.

"Sir, are you all right?"

"Of course I am. It's just a little cut." The alcohol left in the bottle made his skin sing. He pulled a handkerchief out of his pocket, distracted by the sight of the blood, and wrapped his hand. Instantly, a bright red spot soaked through the pure white of the handkerchief.

Ezekielturned back to Wild Johnny and, through gritted teeth said, "Let's go get this motherfucker."

Ezekiel, with a fire in his body that had nothing to do with the booze, stamped up the stairs and out of his house. Johnny followed, his Chevy parked up the street at the Methodist Church. Johnny wasn't a churchgoer, but people in town probably thought him a devotee to the Methodist religion.

Johnny hopped in the driver's seat and Ezekiel popped into the passenger seat. "Have you got a gun?" Ezekiel asked. "I don't usually carry one."

"Sure, boss, I've got one. It's a .44 Magnum. Should be enough to handle whatever you've got. It's in the glove box."

Ezekiel opened it and found the gun inside. It almost didn't fit. He pulled it out, liking the weight of it right away. "This is a goddamn gun. Why'd you need one so big?"

Wild Johnny shrugged. "I'm not a great shot, but that's guaranteed to do some damage no matter where you hit the target."

Ezekiel chuckled. "That why they call you 'Wild'?"

"Something like that."

The truth was, Ezekiel knew, that "Wild" was the moniker that Johnny created for himself. His whole life he wanted to be considered the dangerous one, but no one ever thought of him that way. So he always sought to prove himself as the wild one. Calling himself "Wild" earned him nothing, but performing stupid stunts and nearly getting himself killed, did. He didn't want to do the stunts, he wasn't good at them and he didn't enjoy doing them, but it earned him respect. It also eventually led to his start in crime and organized crime. It wasn't an easy task but he worked his way up to become the right-hand man of the most powerful crime lord in Northwest Oklahoma. Maybe not extreme, but definitely a start.

The car lurched to a stop in front of Hank's house, out on west Cherry Street. "We're damn near out of town." Ezekiel opened the car door and climbed out.

Billy West stood on the porch smoking a cigarette and staring out at the road. It fell from his mouth when Ezekiel and Johnny stepped from the car.

"Brother Ezekiel? What're you doing here? Is that Johnny you're with?"

Ezekiel smiled his brightest smile and stepped onto the porch. "Billy West, didn't you know that Wild Johnny Tompkins is a born-again Christian? He loves the Lord more than you love the booze." He let out a fake, raucous laughter that melted away the moment he pulled the gun from behind his back and pressed the barrel to Billy's head.

Billy's eyes darted up to the gun then down to Ezekiel's then back to the gun. "Brother Ezekiel? That a fake gun?"

"Don't you just wish that it was? Now hand your piece to Johnny."

He reached into his waistband and pulled out a small pistol. His hand trembled as he handed it over to Johnny. "Oh God, I'm going to die, aren't I?"

"Oh, Billy, what would I gain by killing you? But seriously, you didn't learn your lesson when I stopped by your place, did you?"

"I…er…didn't know. I didn't know who you were."

Ezekiel slapped his open palm across Billy's face. The man stumbled back into the wall, holding his reddening cheek. "Take us inside, Billy."

"Yes, sir." It was nearly inaudible through his sobs.

He opened the door to the house and led the preacher in. Hank Thomas sat in an overstuffed chair reading a book, his left arm in a cast. He didn't look up when the three walked in, but continued reading until he finished the page. Once he had, he replaced his bookmark, removed his reading glasses, and closed the book. "I apologize for making you wait, but I do hate when someone interrupts Mark Twain."

When he finally looked up, his eyes grew large enough that he wouldn't need glasses for reading. They darted from Billy to Ezekiel to the gun between them. Ezekiel kicked the backs of Billy's knees so that he knelt in front of him. That made Hank's wandering eyes stop and focus on him. Billy continued blubbering.

"You?" was all Hank could manage to say.

"Hello, Hank, haven't seen you in church lately, so thought I'd make a house visit."

Hank lost the power of speech, his wide eyes taking in the entire scene before him.

Ezekiel pointed the gun at the back of Billy's head and said, "Hey, Billy, are you forgiven?"

"What?" He trembled and cried. It was clear that

Billy did not want to die.

"Are you forgiven?"

"Yes, yes, I am."

Ezekiel smiled. "Then I baptize you in the name of the Father, the Son, and the Holy Spirit." And he pulled the trigger.

The gun boomed through the small house. Most of Billy's head flew in pieces; blood and gore were tossed like celebration confetti. It took a moment for the ringing to clear their ears.

Ezekiel approached Hank, training the gun on him. "You do know you're in trouble, don't you, Hank?"

"My God. You can't do this. You're a preacher." His words came out strained, full of fear.

"That's precisely why I *can* do it. I don't like to see anyone get cheated, Hank, especially not me. And here you are, trying to build up your little booze empire, and I just can't let it happen. Do you have any idea how hard I had to work to get to my position? How many bodies I've had to hide and the terrible time I've had keeping my public and private lives separate? It has been a long journey and I'm not about to let you fuck it up for me."

"Now, wait, Brother Ezekiel, surely we can work something out." He attempted to stand and Ezekiel pushed him back in his seat. Falling jarred his broken arm, and he grabbed at it in pain.

Ezekiel brought the gun down and pressed it to the man's forehead. The barrel was still hot from the bullet that had just left it, but Hank did not shy away from it. Ezekiel said, "Say something good to me, say it now or let your brains decorate that wall, if you have any."

"Wait. You've gotta wait. I can make booze for you."

"I tried that, remember? I wanted you to come to me without the terror. Now your booze won't taste the same because it will have all that fear mixed in with it."

"I can give you my recipe."

Ezekiel pulled the gun back and eyed the coward in front of him. "Get it."

Hank stepped gingerly around the remains of his employee and approached his desk on the opposite side of the room. He walked up to the wall behind his desk and pulled a painting of a black rose from the wall. Behind it was a small safe not unlike the small safe in Ezekiel's home office. He spun the dial three times and opened the door. A small battered paper and a roll of bills was all that was in the safe. Ezekiel thought it too flashy to be his only safe in the house.

Hank grabbed up the paper, hesitated a moment then grabbed the roll of bills. He turned around and handed both to Ezekiel. The preacher weighed the money in his hand then tossed it to Johnny. He took a look at the wrinkled paper. It was indeed a recipe for moonshine, whether it was the exact recipe remained to be seen.

"This really it?"

"Of course. I may have to tweak it from time to time if the ingredients aren't all there, but yes, that's it. What more do you want from me?"

"I'm not sure. I wanted you to come work for me. Wild Johnny over here just could not tempt you or threaten you enough to get you on our team."

"I will. I'll come work for you now. We can forget all this."

"And forget about the bloodstain spreading across your living room floor? I don't know that Billy would appreciate that. He liked you, remember? He chose you."

"I can't help that. I can't change any of it now. Please. I don't want to die tonight."

Ezekiel lifted the gun, stared down the barrel at his last competition in this town, and said, "When do you want to die?"

The blast from the gun didn't seem as loud as the first one, but it did just as much damage, tearing half of Hank's face away, the fear still visible on the other side. His body dropped in slow motion as yet more blood spread across the floor of Hank's house.

Ezekiel turned back to Johnny and tossed him the gun. "I want you to make sure there's no one else here. Find anyone, you kill them. You'll also want to call in the crew and make these bodies disappear."

"Where should we put them, boss?"

"In the river for all I care. Just get them out of this house, and don't bury them in the yard. That'll be the first place someone will look."

Johnny's eyes darted between the two bodies as he contemplated the perfect place to dump them. "Want me to drive you home?"

"No. I'll take a long walk. It'll help to clear my head." He shook it. "That damn booze did a number on me. Just hope I'm not hungover tomorrow."

Chapter 14

Nigel

Nigel finally got the call he'd been waiting for since the election of Governor Edmondson, the call that meant he'd be a part of the task force created by the new governor to enforce prohibition to ensure its removal.

The heels of Nigel's shoes tapped out the rhythm of his steps in the echoing chamber of the interior of the capitol building. A few cleaning ladies could be seen here and there, but the rest of the place seemed as dead as the Indians who once lived here.

A small meeting room on the second floor had been reserved for the task force. Nigel was the third to arrive. He was pleased to see two other officers he knew from the Oklahoma City area. He nodded to them before taking his seat.

They waited twenty minutes and the room slowly filled with officers from all parts of the state. There were thirty total and it was only a moment after the last arrived that the governor walked in. He wore his typical suit and smirk with his hair swept back from his head in a style Elvis might admire. He cleared his throat.

"Thank you, gentlemen, for coming tonight. I know it was short notice and many of you had to drive a few miles to get here." He paused to gaze around the room. "The plan is simple. We have to put a stop to the illegal booze in Oklahoma. I know it seems a large and ridiculous task, but it can be done. Okies will continue to buy illegal booze as long as we let them. And we will never earn a vote from them if it means higher taxes on what they're getting cheap from their neighbors.

"Now, does anyone have any ideas on how to tackle this problem?"

One officer raised his hand. "It really is just a matter of finding out who's making it and shutting them down."

Edmondson nodded. "That's the first step. But not all is coming from local people making it. The border states all legalized booze years ago."

Another officer: "We set up roadblocks on major highways coming into our state. Some will still get through, but that would put a damper on things."

"Excellent thinking. Why don't you head that up?"

Nigel watched the proceedings and realized if he wanted to find out what was happening in the northwest part of the state, this would be his chance. He raised his hand.

"Sir, I'm Inspector Nigel Baxter with OKCPD. I've been studying a map of the state that shows the largest amount of illegal alcohol sales, at least the nearest we can tell. It appears that aside from Oklahoma City and Tulsa, the northwest part of the state is the third largest. And even some of the numbers coming back on that are higher than Tulsa. Something strange seems to be going on there."

Edmondson thought about Nigel's information. "Well, Inspector Baxter, I don't know anyone better to investigate than the man who discovered it. Pack your bags. I'll send word to your supervisor that you're now working for me."

Nigel nodded and smiled. The rest of the meeting went much the same way, with other enforcement being set up around the state. Nigel had a good feeling about the way this would go once he moved.

Chapter 15

Robert

Robert's rebellious spirit hadn't gone away. Not yet. Even if his relationship with his father had improved a great deal since starting his Sunday afternoons with Brother Ezekiel. Oftentimes, those afternoons made him feel better about his impulses instead of worse. It surprised him that church could make him feel so guilty but meeting with the preacher made him feel fine.

Things with Becky had gone from casual to hot and heavy. Everything about her caused him to want to abandon all beliefs about sex being reserved for marriage. She felt quite the same way, and yet they still weren't quite ready to take that next step.

It was a topic that Robert had broached with the preacher on more than one occasion and the two had discussed the repercussions of sex before marriage, and while the church had a definite stance on it, the preacher did not. He'd even gone so far as to say, "As long you're careful and you confess, I don't think there will be an issue." Of course, this was not something that Robert shared with his father.

Then on February 3, 1959, Robert got home from school, ready to do his homework and his chores and try his best to not think about Becky. But when he walked in the front door his mom was sitting there waiting for him.

"Robert, come in here and sit down, please." She spoke the words softly, and he knew that something terrible had happened.

"What is it, Mom?" He tried to keep his mind in check as it raced over all the things she could want to talk to him about. His muscles spasmed uncontrollably.

"Please sit." Lucy rarely sat and had heart-to-hearts with her son. That alone caused alarm in Robert. But also the fact that she was here when Robert, who usually had the house to himself for a couple hours after school, got home. Robert sat.

"Mom, what's going on?" he asked, his voice shaky.

"I wanted to tell you before your father got home. There was a plane crash this morning."

"A plane crash?" Who did he know who'd been on a plane? He couldn't think of anyone.

"Ritchie Valens and the Big Bopper were on it," she said, tears welling up in her eyes. "And so was Buddy Holly."

The news broke over him, first relieving him because he wasn't in trouble, and then breaking him apart. He couldn't fathom the talented singer being ripped from the world so soon. He was only twenty-three, for crying out loud. He couldn't be dead. He found he couldn't respond to his mom, but just sat shaking his head; tears falling onto his upturned palms seemed to come from nowhere.

Lucy hugged him, rocking him gently from side to side and whispering, "I know," to him over and over. He allowed himself to be held, trying to blink back the tears.

After a few minutes, he calmed down and so, since his dad wasn't home yet, his mom went to his room and grabbed one of his 45's and put it on the family stereo. She'd chosen "Oh Boy!" one of Buddy's most upbeat works. The words came tumbling out of the speakers and Robert hopped up to dance away his sadness.

The words struck home with Robert as he danced, and he suddenly had to make sure he could see Becky tonight. So while his mom continued to dance, he stepped from the room to quickly call her to make plans. She wanted to be with him after learning of Buddy Holly's death and told him she would do whatever she could to get out of the house. Before getting off the phone, he said the two lines from "Oh Boy!" to her.

He borrowed his dad's truck under the premise of running into town to work on a homework assignment with a friend of his named William. William also attended the First Baptist Church and was a member of the youth group. Robert didn't like him much, but their family didn't have a phone so he couldn't call when he got there to prove his whereabouts. It was a good alibi. And even though it was a Tuesday night, his father let him go.

Becky climbed into the cab wearing a black skirt with a white blouse. Fortunately the heater in the truck worked well so the cold air that came in with Becky was quickly forgotten. Robert's eyes went instantly to the swell of her breasts that caused a tingling deep between his legs. He popped the truck into gear as Becky slid over in the seat next to him. Between gears, his hand found her bare leg and slid a little higher each time.

Once at their spot, Becky leaned into his neck and began to kiss him. He felt himself go hard as his fingertips brushed the edge of her panties. She slid her left leg against his and her right leg as far from her body as she could, opening a new world to him.

Words didn't need to come between them, not tonight. They simply needed each other in a way they'd never experienced. Because of the lyrics, she knew that tonight was the night, so where she would normally pull away, now she would yield, giving herself over to him completely.

Their clothes fell from their bodies easier than the guilt would later. Their breath, combined with the cold of the night air, fogged the inside of the windows.

Robert felt the heat of her skin as she climbed on top of him. Her hair hung down and tickled his cheeks and they never stopped kissing each other. The moments passed in that manner, with tenderness and pent-up aggression. It was better than Robert had expected. It was being told about the sunset then seeing it with your own eyes. All he'd ever heard about sex was wrong, or not quite enough.

Afterwards, he thought of the many missed opportunities the two had had to explore this wild and new adventure. He also wondered how he would ever face his mother and father again. He was sure they would be able to see something different in him, something that would make him stand out from the virgins around him.

"Thank you," he whispered to her.

Her forehead, damp with sweat, rested against his own. "Thank you."

"Can you believe it?"

"No, I can't."

He'd prepared for the event, reading up about sex, and had brought a towel. From what he understood, there was a lot of blood when a woman lost her virginity. He was surprised to find none when they turned on the dome light to find their clothes. "Huh," he said.

"What?" she asked as she pulled her white panties back on, her bare breasts exposed to the inside of the truck and Robert's wandering eyes.

"There's no blood." He held up the towel to show her.

"Oh." She turned her head away from him. "I may have broken that already, a couple weeks ago."

"Oh."

She turned her head back to him. "Yeah."

He leaned into her, taking a breast in his hand and kissing her. He found the idea of her exploring her own body terribly exciting. Ten minutes after their first time, they experienced their second time. It wasn't a magical event worth writing books about, but for them, it was good.

When he dropped her off at her house, she stopped before getting out. "Are we going to regret this?"

He sighed. "God, I hope not."

She smiled. "Me too. I really enjoyed myself."

"As did I. My biggest concern right now is when we can do it again."

This time she laughed. "I think I love you, Robert. And I don't want things to be weird because of that, but it's true. You've really brightened my life these last few months, and I see only good things in the future for us."

His cheeks warmed and the smile dropped from his face. "I think I love you, too." He shook his head. "No, I *know* I do."

She smiled. "Good." She leaned across the seat to give him one more kiss. "And I better be the only one."

He lay awake in bed that night staring at his ceiling, thinking of her. The girl he'd thought of for months and months, and he knew would continue to think of for many, many more months to come. He believed that Sunday would be a tough day, but he suspected something good would come from his afternoon meeting with the preacher.

Still, the images of Rebecca Lewis wandered through his mind and he felt a stiffening between his legs. He reached his hand under the covers to test how much stamina he had.

Chapter 16

Ezekiel

That Sunday, a new man walked through the doors of the First Baptist Church. Of course, Ezekiel noticed him immediately as he stood before his congregation and welcomed them to another fine Sunday morning. His sermon that day focused on the book of Genesis, going back to the very beginning of it all: man, woman, and sin. With his alcohol sales at an all-time high, he saw no reason to be over the top talking about the alcohol again. There was no way prohibition would end. Oklahomans wanted their booze, and they wanted it cheap, without the taxes the government would impose on it.

But there, in the center section of his church, sat this stranger. A fedora rested on the pew next to him and rimless glasses perched on top of his nose with a neatly trimmed mustache under it. He appeared to be in his late forties but could have been as old as sixty. Ezekiel didn't like the sight of him for whatever reason. A dread seemed to build in his gut because of the man.

In all frankness, he looked like a cop. And not one of the cops around town that he knew to accept bribes of cash and booze.

After the sermon, Ezekiel stood in his customary place in the foyer, shaking hands with his flock and smiling appreciatively at the compliments of his sermon.

The man came through the line and shook his hand.

"I don't know that I've seen you here," Ezekiel said. The man had a thin hand with well-manicured fingernails. Upon closer inspection, the preacher decided he must be closer to sixty.

"Well, I'm new around here. I've already heard great things about this church, though, so I thought I would try it out. I must say I was not disappointed."

"The good Lord smiles down on us, that is for sure. But please, tell me your name."

"Oh sure." He reached into his jacket and pulled a business card from his inner pocket. "I'm Nigel Baxter, the new chief investigator in the northwest part of Oklahoma."

Ezekiel read the business card and saw nothing good on it. "And what is it you're investigating?"

Nigel smiled. "I don't know if you have plans for lunch, but I would like to buy you a meal if I could."

A cold sweat broke out on Ezekiel's skin, but he responded, "Sir, that would be lovely."

After the church crowd made their exit, and the few stragglers, those asking for a word of prayer or a word of support for some imagined difficult time, finally left, Ezekiel climbed into the black state-issued sedan of Nigel Baxter. They made their way two blocks north to a small diner located downtown on the west side of the Square. The church-goers, Methodist and Baptist alike, made the walls feel a little closer, but Ezekiel and Nigel found a booth in the corner of the place that was unoccupied. A harried looking waitress took their order and brought them each a cup of coffee. They sipped the coffee in silence, Ezekiel waiting for the new man to break the silence.

"The place is packed. It must be good."

"That it is," Ezekiel said, "But as long as I let church out before the Methodists across the street, we get the good seats." The two laughed cheerfully and conversation turned to that of the town, the new home to Nigel.

Over the next few minutes, the stranger gave little information about himself. So when their food arrived, along with a coffee refill, the preacher finally had to ask, "So what is it you're investigating?"

Nigel took a moment to answer, swallowing the big bite of sandwich he'd taken. "Something sinister is growing under the surface of your fine town, sir. I'm here to find the source and eradicate it." He took another bite.

Ezekiel watched him eat, unsure how to respond. The man clearly had a hearty appetite and spoke in cryptic messages. Ezekiel didn't take his eyes off Mr. Baxter as he ate his own sandwich.

When the two men had finally finished lunch, Nigel pulled a pack of cigarettes out of the inner pocket of his suit. He offered one to Ezekiel but he declined. With fresh smoke hanging over them, Nigel said, "You probably have more questions, but I appreciate that you waited until after the meal. I prefer to save my conversation for after I eat."

Ezekiel inclined his head, accepting the thanks even if he hadn't done it to be respectful. "Your statement left me a little dumbfounded, I guess."

"And I thought that it might. What I mean to say is that the governor of our fine state is using his resources to locate the weak spots in an age-old law."

"Are you referring to prohibition?"

Nigel smiled, took another drag. "You're catching

on. From what I understand, he's going to enforce it so that he can end it. Interesting concept. But as we all know, Okies won't vote to end it if they can get the booze cheaper with it in place."

"And that's where you come in?"

"That's where I come in. I'm covering all of the northwestern part of the state, and I suppose, the panhandle. I'm sure out here I'll find less bootlegging and more runs into different states. But I shouldn't jump to conclusions, should I?"

Ezekiel didn't move, but he could feel himself smiling at the statement. He clutched his arm to keep his hand from wiping at the beads of sweat that popped suddenly up on his forehead. He cleared his throat. "You really believe alcohol is a problem here?"

"Mr. Wilson, with all due respect, you've preached on the subject more times than I care to count. Surely you suspect something."

Ezekiel's eyebrows shot up.

"Don't worry about it. I made it a point to do a little research before coming here. That's why I wanted to meet with you. Personally I'm a Methodist." He held up his hands. "I know, I am the enemy." They both laughed. "But I must say, you seem to have a real passion for prohibition and the refraining from alcoholic beverages. I like that."

Ezekiel didn't have to fake this smile. "I am a Baptist minister. Aren't we all that way?"

Nigel leaned forward across the table, the smoke from his cigarette drifting lazily into Ezekiel's nostrils. "You'd be surprised. Oughta head down to the City some time and see what they're saying down there. Yes, sir, it would make most Baptist ministers turn cold at the words, but they're the ones saying it." He shook his head. "I don't know what this country is coming to, but I will say that I'm here to uphold the law and that is something I cannot fail to do."

Ash drifted off the end of Nigel's cigarette and landed in the small ashtray on the table between them. Ezekiel watched it fall, seeing his empire reflected there.

"I do not want to see prohibition end. I know many of my flock have a difficult struggle with the drink. I often have ten to twenty during the altar call confess their sins with it. I believe the booze allows many to do things they would never do under normal circumstances. What good could possibly come from making the thing legal?"

"I have no opinion, but surely with that many admitting to their sins, you can see what a problem alcohol is here. Personally, I like a good beer from time to time and the 'non-intoxicating' stuff sold in this state hits the spot just fine. If the hard stuff is legalized, I will still have my beer from time to time and others will have whatever it is they like. The only difference is the state will see some more income with the taxation of the alcohol. I kind of like that idea."

Ezekiel nodded as Nigel snubbed out his cigarette in the ashtray on the table. "I am not against the state getting more money, but I am against people getting more booze. If you can stop the inflow of alcohol, maybe everyone will see the real purpose of prohibition and will then accept it."

Nigel chuckled. "If you want to hope for that, go ahead. I can guarantee you this though: I will catch anyone smuggling or making alcohol. And they will go away for a long time, I can assure you."

****

“These days have not been easy, and I fear that there are still many difficult days ahead of us.” Ezekiel paused and sipped his water. It was tepid, but he didn’t mind. He’d worked over this speech again and again, wondering exactly how to deal it out. “A generous donor has seen it fit to give us a substantial amount of money that will help us to climb out of the debt we’ve found ourselves in.”

He paused, allowing for the obligatory “Amens” that would come from the devoutly hopeful in his audience. The church was near to full this morning. It seemed the rumors of the demise of the Baptist church had floated easily around the town like a log down a river. Ezekiel hoped that his words this morning might release a few more dollars from the pockets of all these curious.

“I will admit that when I saw the size of the offering, I nearly fell over. There will be a golden castle in Heaven for anyone as generous as that. And I know that many of you are ready to get home and call the donor in the hopes of giving the loudest thanks and praises, however that is not possible. The offering was given anonymously.

“That does not mean that we should not be thankful, of course, but that we should turn our thanks and praises to Heaven. Who will join me this morning in praising our Lord?”

It was not quite the Baptist way to cheer in church, however theirs was the loudest “Amen” he’d ever heard. He bowed his head and closed his eyes and prayed a sincerely earnest prayer. He hadn’t felt this relieved since coming to this town. At the end of the prayer, he stole a glance at his wife, sitting prettily on the front pew of the church. Without her, he knew he would be lost.

In the days following her idea, they had gotten to work quickly. He'd never really touched alcohol, having no interest in it, and Mary hadn't had a drink since high school. They had a lot of learning to do as they brought her uncle to town to help in the creation of their first batch of booze.

Little by little, they got better, and began selling their mason jars to those who needed it. A slight pang of guilt tugged at Ezekiel as the first people they sold to were some who'd come to him Sunday mornings for prayer. However, he saw the needs of the church greater than the parts. They sold entirely through Mary's uncle instead of risking exposure in town for what they were doing in secret.

Shortly after the sales began in earnest, Mary's uncle approached Ezekiel. "I've got someone to introduce to you."

The man had to be near seventy, his skin dried leather that had been hardened by the sun and a hard life. The man's name was Rodney Ericson. "I don't know you, and you don't know me, but you better watch your step. You've been selling and there's several people already in this town who want to enjoy the profits. You're infringing."

At the time, Ezekiel kept books in a small house over on High Street where their still was set up. He sat back in his chair and gave Rodney's words some real thought. Finally he said, "How much moonshine do you make a week?"

Rodney laughed, something that sounded more like he was clearing phlegm out of his throat. "Why would I tell you that? What business is it of yours?"

Ezekiel scratched at a spot on his forearm. "What

business is it of yours what we're doing here?"

"I'm not saying it is. I'm simply giving you a piece of advice."

"And I'm going to give you one: you can either start working for me, or you can continue to lose all of your profits."

Rodney's mouth fell open, and Ezekiel could see all of his rotted teeth floating next to his fat tongue.

"Mr. Ericson, you'd be foolish to turn down anything. I'm giving you the opportunity to make more money than you ever have in the moonshine business. Our customer base is growing daily and we're having trouble keeping up."

Ezekiel glanced over at his wife who winked at him. Their customer base was not, in fact, that big; however, Rodney didn't know that. But it could be with Rodney's customers.

That was how Ezekiel got his first employee outside of family. Before he stood in front of his church on that Sunday, he managed to snag one more moonshiner to his side. The added revenue from the additional moonshiners left him with enough profits to slip it to the church as an anonymous donation to help get the church out of the hole.

"You're quite the business man," Mary said to him on more than one occasion. It was a fair statement. He'd managed to, in just a few weeks, move their operation to something that had paid employees and brought in a great deal of money. The word got around quickly that their product was the best one.

And the secret of Ezekiel's identity remained secret until someone got jealous of his success.

Chapter 17

Nigel

After lunch, Nigel drove aimlessly, just passing through the neighborhoods and enjoying the sights of his little city. So far, he liked it and thought it a good place to live, at least it would be when he got it cleaned up.

He lit a cigarette, the smoke hanging around the inside of the car like the three-day stubble that hung around his face. It was a beautiful day, one of the warmest days this winter, a hint of the coming spring. He had to report to the governor's office later, but for now, he wanted to simply enjoy the day.

He let his thoughts wander back over his conversation with the preacher. The man seemed stubborn on the subject of prohibition. He understood it was part of the rhetoric of the Baptists to condemn drinking while at church and condone it in private; at least that was always the joke. Still he thought the end of prohibition was a good thing with the increased flow of money from taxes and the decreased amount of people serving jail sentences from something that's legal in forty-six of the forty-eight other states.

Nigel had always been somewhat progressive in his thinking, however, and he understood that not everyone felt the way did; he didn't know why they didn't, but he allowed that that was something that tended to happen.

After meeting with the preacher, Nigel knew he would be quintessential in eradicating alcohol. He'd been consistent in preaching against it and praying for forgiveness for those that did partake, no matter how many times they asked for it. Typically, Mr. Nigel Baxter could be found amongst the patrons of the First United Methodist Church of Oklahoma City. However, he thought the ideals expressed by the Baptist church when it came to alcohol would be more helpful. His church family, as they called it, would probably melt if they entered a Baptist church. Many among them still held firm to the division between the churches. Yet again, Nigel was progressive in his beliefs.

Watching the town pass before him, Nigel felt he could begin to understand it a little better. Here and there were some rough buildings and houses. The north side of town was the most rundown, but still, he saw no homeless. A rundown house was better than no house, he supposed. Plenty of large houses dotted the sides of the streets, places that looked like they might be at home in Heritage Hills down in OKC.

He went south on Fourteenth Street, his old car climbing the big hill. He passed the hospital, a blond brick affair that was at least three stories, likely with a basement. Nigel didn't like it and said a silent prayer that he wouldn't have to see the inside of it.

The big water tower on the Boulevard said the only thing anyone driving through might need to know: the town's name. He barely glanced at it as he headed east back toward the college where he could turn back to the north and back to the police station. He had to type up that report, his initial reaction to the town, and have his secretary call the governor's office to give the report.

All in all, he decided, it wasn't a bad town, just another place. Likely there was no alcohol here, at least no more than most towns. He hummed a hymn from that morning and tapped his steering wheel in time with the tune.

Chapter 18

Robert

Despite the mild weather outside, Robert and Ezekiel sat in his living room, each holding a glass of iced tea. The amber liquid quenched the thirst you would never know you had unless you drank it. But once tasted, it could never be turned down. These were not quite the thoughts Robert had as he took a swig of his tea; he would never be that poetic.

Silence settled over the room in the moments since the preacher had gotten their tea. The only sound, aside from the ice cubes clinking against the side of the glass, was the ticking of a clock. Brother Ezekiel didn't speak or touch his tea, but instead stared off into the distance and ran his hands through his hair.

Robert planned on telling Ezekiel about his sexual escapades with Becky, but he didn't want to be the one who broached the subject. He liked for Ezekiel to be the one to ask questions.

So he waited. When he had nearly finished his glass, Ezekiel spoke, "I do apologize, young Bobby, but I seem to have a lot on my mind today."

"That's fine, sir. I can come back another time if I need to." He stood, ready to carry his glass back into the kitchen.

Ezekiel waved the idea away. "Don't be silly.

You're here. Sit down and we can talk. But if I seem to be lost in thought, it's nothing you've done."

"Is there anything I can do to help, sir?"

He smiled. "No, Bobby. I met the new investigator for the alcohol problem around here this morning. He seems to have a promising idea of what he wants to do to help."

"Well, that's great, isn't it?"

"Sure it is. Except that many of my flock are haunted by the evils of alcohol and I wouldn't want to see any of them with criminal charges brought against them."

"That makes sense, I guess. But couldn't that help them? I mean, if the new guy was able to find the source of the alcohol then they wouldn't be able to get it, right?"

"That's true, but what if there isn't a source for it? What if they're just making their way into Kansas to get their booze?"

"I hadn't thought of that."

"I know. I worry too much." He sighed and grabbed up his own glass. In one swallow, half of it was gone. "So tell me what it is that you want to talk about today?"

Robert cleared his throat, shifted the tea glass from hand to hand, the bits of ice left in it swimming from side to side. He adjusted his legs and fidgeted with his pant leg. Finally he met the preacher's eyes. "I didn't think this would be so hard." He gave a humorless chuckle and swallowed. "I lost my virginity this week."

"I see. How do you feel now?"

"Scared and a little guilty, I suppose. I don't regret it though, that's the weird part. I was sure I would regret it."

Ezekiel nodded. "That makes sense. It is quite the experience. In some ways it changes things for the bad and in others, it can change them for the good. But it does change things, you must be sure of that. Where do you go from here?"

"Sir?"

"What I mean is: do you continue to have sex or do you chalk it up as an experience and move on?"

"I hadn't thought that far ahead. I don't know that I would be able to stop myself from doing it again."

"Therein lies the problem. The Bible has a great deal to say on the subject of sex and sex before marriage, but I won't bore you with a thousand-year old book."

Robert's eyes shot wide at that statement; he thought it the sole desire of preachers to quote the Good Book.

Ezekiel continued, "I've known plenty of people who've had sexual experiences outside of the confines of marriage, and it always has different side effects. But the most consistent one is, once you've done it, you can never undo it. There is a reason that there's a word to describe someone who hasn't yet had sex, as opposed to a word to describe someone who has. The word virgin carries a lot of weight to it."

Robert's whole body warmed and leaned back in his chair, mouth wide open.

"I'm not trying to guilt you, I'm simply stating facts. Sex will change everything, but hopefully only for the better." The preacher cleared his throat. "What I mean to say is, did you have sex because you love the girl and you wanted to express that love physically or was it some other reason? Maybe a combination of reasons?"

Robert shifted some more and felt those cold prickles of sweat on his forehead he'd gotten used to feeling on these Sunday visits. "I do love her, but I would be wrong to say that that's the only reason."

"So what other reason is there?"

"I knew that my dad would hate it if he found out about it. I don't know. That made it more taboo and desirable. He's been really riding me a lot lately."

"Bobby, that is very…grown-up of you to admit. Most who rebel do so because of the temptation to do something forbidden. That's half the fun, isn't it? Your understanding of that is impressive."

"Thank you, sir. Does this mean I can still go to Heaven?"

Ezekiel thought that over for a second. "I've said on Sunday mornings that eternity is not something that God will give you and then take away. Once you are saved, you are always saved. You've been forgiven for all of your sins, including those you haven't committed yet. I don't think you have anything to worry about."

Robert's face split into a huge grin. "Hearing that takes a world of pressure off of me. I've been feeling sure this sin was a spit in the face of God and He would reject me for it."

"I don't presume to know the thoughts of God, but what I do know about Him comes from His Word and that gives no indication that God would abandon you, especially when you need him."

The rest of the afternoon slipped by in peace with good conversation. Ezekiel even seemed to be getting over the funk he'd been in when Robert first arrived.

After Robert got home that evening, he saw the world a little differently, like he was above it and saw everything from a different angle than most saw it. Either that or he was living ten seconds in the future and could see things happening before they happened. He felt detached from the world he'd always known.

"What did you and the preacher talk about this week?" Mike asked when he got home. Lucy brought her eyes up from the pile of socks she was darning. She always showed Robert a great deal of interest when he returned from the preacher's house.

This was the last thing Brother Ezekiel and Robert discussed each week: what to say to Mike when he got home. They planned it out so that their stories would match.

"This week we spoke of the dangers of women. He's helped me to understand the burden of man. We have a privilege to take care of the women in our world and messing them up by convincing them to lie and sneak out will only hurt them in the long run. It was a helpful conversation."

Mike smiled. "I sure appreciate the changes I'm seeing in you each week. You've dropped all the rebelliousness, done chores without a second thought, and you've been reading your Bible in the living room and asking questions about certain passages. I can say that I'm glad for these meetings you've had with Ezekiel. Maybe I should send your mom to visit with him, too." He laughed, but when Robert looked at his mom to see her reaction, he was surprised to see her cheeks were quite red. His dad didn't notice.

Mike picked up his crossword he'd been working on when Robert got home. "There's some trash out in the pit that needs to be burned. Do that for me, then get upstairs and work on your homework."

"Yes, sir."

Robert walked out back to the pit and saw the pile of garbage waiting for the flame. Charles stood next to it, waiting for him.

"I wanted to watch the fire burn, boy," he said. "Hope that's okay with you."

"That's fine. What's not fine is you calling me 'boy' again."

"Oh right. I forgot about that. Wanna prove you're not a boy?" He pulled a small glass bottle from his coat and tossed it to him. "Drink that."

Robert caught it and stared down at it, his heart a kick drum in his chest. He shrugged, twisted off the cap, and experienced a second first that weekend.

Chapter 19

Robert

The effects of alcohol were quick for someone who had never experienced it. The only reason Robert decided to pop the top of the bottle and drink was to impress Charles. The night of Robert's first drink loosened Robert's tongue so that Charles became the second person to hear the story of his sexual exploits. He'd told, and in the process, gained a new respect in his father's hired hand.

For the next week, Robert was drunk whenever he could be without worrying about his father finding out. Working chores around the farm kept him out of the house and out with Charles who would supply the booze. Robert never asked where he got it, but found himself enjoying it more and more. It seemed that each swallow of the liquid pushed the guilt while the memory of his time with Becky remained fully intact.

The next Sunday afternoon, Robert confessed his latest transgression to the preacher. Ezekiel Wilson once more absolved him of the sins, and while he didn't exactly encourage the drinking, he didn't discourage it either.

Now Robert felt better than ever about life after his Sunday afternoon visits with the preacher. He no longer harbored the guilt that he once did. His behavior at school and at home was basically the same as it had been, but he would now sneak a cigarette, kiss Becky when no one was looking, drink booze-laced soda at school. His masturbation had also increased to new levels after his experience with Becky. All he had to do was imagine the hem of her skirt and he was ready.

The Monday after his most recent meeting with the preacher, Becky and Robert were able to steal away after school so that he could see her breasts in the afternoon sun. The experience was better than the first to the point that if it continued to get better, Robert saw no way that he could ever stop. He brought a jar of moonshine, really strong stuff he'd gotten from Charles, and the two had taken deep drinks of it before and after their deed. Robert knew that he was a different person than the one Becky had first gone out with, but he also knew this new version of him tended to turn her on.

Sitting on the towel that he always brought along, his seed dripping onto it between her legs, she drank from the jar again and said, "I'm feeling rather light-headed."

"That from the booze or me?" He pulled from the moonshine himself, happy to see that he wasn't feeling its effects nearly as much as he had that first night.

"Both, I think. Do you ever feel we shouldn't be doing any of this?"

He put the lid on the jar, giving her question a lot of honest thought. "I don't. I'm in love with you, Becky, and I've never felt so free and full of life."

Her face broke into a genuine grin. "You're in love with me?"

His eyes darted from the afternoon sunlight, to her face, and back again. "Yes. I've questioned the existence of God many times in my life, but I will never question my love for you. You occupy all of my thoughts to the point that I have no room for anything else. Becky, if I could marry you right now, I would."

The words were like lemonade on a hot summer day. She leaned into him, their bare skin sending electrical charges through their bodies. "And I'm in love with you. Marry me when you can, Robert Arrington, I will wait for you."

It seemed the greatest time of Robert's life was beginning at last. He would soon learn the bitter taste of life, however, and he would begin to look on these days with longing and regret.

Chapter 20

Ezekiel

Her smile was much the same as it had been all those years ago, her body slightly older, but then so was his. For all the problems in the world, Ezekiel's time with Lucy was among the greatest moments he could experience. He knew he would never love her, at least not the way he loved Mary, but he did have a deep desire for companionship. And really he wasn't entirely convinced Lucy could ever love him. Not that she loved Mike either.

Ezekiel shook his head to get all the thoughts out and focus on the moment. Lucy had come over to have some alone time with him, and he would take advantage of it all.

Her dress lay in a crumpled heap on the floor next to the bed. He barely had time to get his pants off before she was on top of him, wrestling his underwear down his legs. It was good to be wanted.

Afterward, he lay in a pool of sunlight that may have come directly from Heaven. In moments of pure bliss like this, Ezekiel could remember exactly what he felt in the presence of God back when he believed with his whole being.

"You know what we should do?" Lucy asked, her voice thick like wool.

"What's that?" Ezekiel stared up at the cracked, white ceiling. He knew what she would say before she said it. Sex often ended with this conversation.

"We should run away. I could leave Mike, you know I could."

"Hmmm." Thoughts entered Ezekiel's brain of Mike's smug face, of Lucy's son, and then of the new inspector who promised to clean up the town. Those three things together put dangerous thoughts in his head. "Maybe we should start thinking about it."

She sat up, wide-eyed. "You're serious?"

He sat up and grabbed her arm gently. "Well, Robert's about to graduate and that governor is promising an end to prohibition, so it makes sense doesn't it?"

She smiled, a genuine beam of sunlight. "Oh, Ezekiel, finally! I've been waiting for so long to leave that man."

"I know."

She leaned in and kissed him.

After that conversation, it seemed that nothing could dampen Lucy's spirit. Ezekiel liked the idea, really, it got him excited. It would cause quite the scandal in this little town if the Baptist preacher ran off with the wife of a Deacon. That alone made him smile.

But the truth was, he loved Lucy about as much as he could. There would never be any replacing Mary, and he thought that deep down, Lucy knew that. But even if she couldn't take that top spot away from her, Lucy was still the top spot of any living woman.

****

During their second year at the church, with the financial woes nearly behind them and big plans ahead of them, Ezekiel and Mary began the excavation of the secret basement room. They had three boys from the church come and help them cart the dirt away, claiming it to be a much-needed renovation. At the time, Ezekiel enjoyed a rather trusting congregation so that he could essentially do what he wanted without a second thought.

Having a place to store the goods near at hand was extremely important. A man named Tom Berlow had robbed nearly three hundred dollars' worth of moonshine from them. Unfortunately, Ezekiel hadn't found out until the man had already hopped a train back to Wichita. He really wanted to send someone to find him to break his hands, but Mary talked him down.

"He just needed it more," she said. "Remember why we're doing this."

It was easy to forget the goodness of the Lord while they were committing crimes. This wasn't quite like the apostles in the book of Acts who were committing the crime of spreading the Gospel, but instead, he was spreading sin to help the Gospel prosper. It didn't make a lot of sense if he thought about it too much.

While finishing the moving of jars to the newly built hidden room, the unthinkable happened. A parishioner from the church came wandering into the house. "Brother Ezekiel? Mary?" They heard the call from up the stairs.

"Is someone in the house?" Mary asked.

Ezekiel just stared back with wide eyes, and he dropped a jar of moonshine that promptly smashed on the ground at his feet. The noise brought the nosey churchgoer to the door of the basement stairs. "Ezekiel, is that you?"

Before the couple could move, someone began

descending the stairs.

"Mary, are you down here?"

Mary and Ezekiel stood rooted to the ground. Fear has a way of freezing those who need to desperately move. They watched as the woman came into view, and Ezekiel knew as soon as he saw her that his life as a pastor had ended.

"There you two are." Lucy smiled. "I've been knocking and when nobody answered, I let myself in. I was afraid that you'd hurt yourselves or something." This was an unfortunate problem they'd had in the past, nearly getting caught in the act of sex by some random and concerned old lady who had nothing better to do. Yet, this was one closer to their own age, one who happened to be married to one of the up and coming farmers of the community.

"Hello, Lucy," Mary said, stepping forward and attempting to block her view of the jars of moonshine scattered around the room.

"What is that smell?" Her nose crinkled like she could hardly breathe.

"I haven't noticed anything." Mary grabbed Lucy's arm and attempted to lead her back up the stairs, but Lucy pulled away.

"What is that stuff?" she asked. "What's in those jars?"

"Nothing, Lucy, come on, I'll get you some tea." Again, Lucy resisted.

"Is that…alcohol?" She whispered the last word as if it might come up and attack her right out of those jars if she said it too loud.

"What? No, Lucy, where would you get that idea?"

"Mary," Ezekiel sighed. "It's okay. I think the jig is

up, as they say."

Mary turned aside and fell into a chair the way Ezekiel's jar had fallen. It all was about to break apart and Ezekiel decided they had to face it.

"Lucy, welcome to our home. I suppose you would like an explanation?"

Lucy's eyes continued to dart around, taking in the contents of all the jars. She paused in her inventory to meet Ezekiel's eyes and she nodded.

Ezekiel sighed again, knowing that telling would be the hardest part, and it would not be the last time he would tell it. "Well, we're running a bit of an illegal bootlegging operation here." He held up his hands as if Lucy was attempting to cut him off. "Now, most of the money we make from this, we give back to the church. Remember that sizable donation from an anonymous donor?"

She nodded.

"That was us."

Mary stood and put her arm gently on Lucy's shoulder. "It was something we knew we could do to save the church. It was near bankruptcy when we got here. We managed to stop that from happening."

Lucy's eyes welled with tears. "I had no idea." Her voice, barely loud enough to hear over the blood rushing in his ears. "I didn't know the church was that bad. I mean, I knew it was bad. We heard too many sermons on tithing and offerings before you came. I think that's why so many people were excited to hear you speak since you had a fresh take on the gospel we hadn't heard in too long.

"And now you've found a way to make money to keep the doors of the church open. And the stuff you're selling is ensuring that more people will need to come to the church to repent of their sins."

She took a deep breath and walked up to Ezekiel. He didn't know what was coming but when she wrapped her arms around him in a tight embrace, he certainly wasn't expecting that. "You're a hero, Brother Ezekiel."

He returned the hug and looked over her shoulder with wide eyes at his wife. When the embrace ended, Lucy asked, "So you need some help around here?"

Chapter 21

Nigel

"Sir, I am the appointed chief of police. I will remain in charge in my own station." Flecks of spit flew off the tongue of Chief Eugene Ross, his red skin taught around his throat as he let loose his torrent of words.

Nigel stood aptly listening, revealing no anger on his own face despite feeling a great deal of it. "I appreciate that, Chief Ross. Yet, while you're appointed by the local mayor, I have been appointed to be here by the governor of our great state. Tell me which you believe trumps the other."

Though his face was still red, Chief Ross let the comment go without responding. Nigel smiled at him and turned back to the few officers in the room with them. "Gentlemen, thank you for being here today. In the last couple months, a suspected moonshiner disappeared. As did a known alcoholic. Along with those disappearances, alcohol sales here are on the rise. At least they must be. I've seen empty jars, cans, and bottles. I've seen plenty of people walking unsteadily, and I've only been here a few days. And yet there have been surprisingly few arrests.

"On top of that, I've thought that we should change our policy of arresting someone and letting them go home the next day. Drinking is against the law and should start to be strictly enforced. We will take back the town from the grasp of booze."

He noticed a couple of the officers unable to make eye contact with him. Bribes were not uncommon in the city, so he'd expected to find some dirty cops here. He just hoped he'd be able to either catch them or encourage them to change their ways. With a surprisingly small number of officers to choose from, he hoped for the latter.

He hadn't meant to have a confrontation with the chief of the town, but when he'd insisted on having a meeting with all of the officers to discuss the illegal alcohol problem, Chief Ross had become incensed, a clear clue to Nigel that the man had his own stake in the moonshine business. A little time and a lot of hard work, and Nigel was certain he would root out any of the officers who had a hand in the illegal activities.

After the meeting, he gave the officers their assignments and decided to get a better feel for the town by visiting houses door to door. He worked the afternoon away, finding plenty of those doors closing in his face. Really the work proved fruitless, with the exception of giving him the ability to see the town a little more and talk to a few people here and there. Without being able to enter people's dwellings and see their things, he couldn't rule out that they were moonshiners. He also couldn't rule them out as homosexuals, Satanists, or pornographic actors.

Winter had held on for far too long. The groundhog had seen his shadow so it wasn't as if this cold weather hadn't been predicted, but still, walking around the town, Nigel wished he'd worn thicker socks.

On the way back to the station, he passed, a small,

red brick house with a single car garage attached to it. The door to the garage was open and a man sat alone in the dark confines of the garage, wrapped in a blanket with a small space heater glowing beside him. Nigel noticed the man held a beer in one hand, and Nigel suddenly had a taste for one.

He meandered up the driveway and spoke with the stranger. "Hello, sir, how are you today?"

The man, who must have been in his fifties, peered up at him, his glasses catching a glint of light. "I'm mighty fine. And how are you?"

Nigel smiled. "Quite well. I wonder if I could join you. I've been wandering the neighborhood and I have developed quite the thirst. And if you wouldn't mind me warming my digits with your heater that would sure be nice."

"I wouldn't say no to that. Have a beer. There's plenty. And hell, I'm starting to sweat a little." He let loose a hardy chuckle and indicated a cooler on the garage floor beside him. Nigel opened it and found at least twenty cans of beer inside. This man was in it for the long hall. He could appreciate that.

Nigel's new friend offered a church key which Nigel used to poke two holes in the top of the can. The taste settled nicely on his tongue and gave him the best feeling he'd had all day. "Where'd you get the beer?" Nigel ventured to ask.

"Like it? I picked that up in Kansas yesterday."

"Kansas?" Nigel peered down at the can in his hand but could find no information regarding the ABV. He assumed it would be considered an intoxicating beverage. "Well, how about that? Make a lot of runs up there?"

"No, sir, I just happened to be up that way, visiting a friend and found that I needed some beer. So I stopped. Didn't have to work today and thought that this would be the best way to spend it."

Nigel glanced around the garage, tools hanging neatly organized from pegs along the walls. One thing was noticeably absent. "Where's the car that would normally be resting here?"

The stranger gave a chuckle. "Noticed that, did you? My wife had some shopping she wanted to do today. Not a lot. Just the usual groceries and errand type of thing. Me not needing the car gave her that opportunity."

Nigel took another drink from the can and discovered it was empty. He tossed it in the trashcan nearby that already had three cans in it. "Name's Nigel Baxter, by the way."

The stranger nodded his head. "Pleased to meet you. I'm Clarence. Clarence Parker. You can have another if you'd like. I've got plenty."

"I saw that. But no thank you. I'm actually working right now."

"Sort of work do you do?"

"I'm the lead investigator for the underground booze in the region. This is the government's attempt to enforce prohibition."

Clarence's eyes got wide. "This is the only time I've ever bought higher point beer, I promise. You have to give me another chance."

Nigel chuckled. "I wouldn't waste my time. Plus I'd have to arrest myself for partaking. No, I'm looking for the real heavy hitters. The ones that make their own with intent to distribute. Know any of them?"

Clarence shook his head. "I don't know much about

the crime syndicate in this town. I enjoy my beer from time to time, but I certainly don't partake in the hard stuff. I've got to go to church on Sunday mornings and face up to my God and this," he indicated the can, "is difficult enough to atone for."

Nigel nodded. "Which church do you attend?"

"I'm a Catholic, born and raised. Got married at the Baptist church though. The wife is a Baptist, which is usually the end, but we've managed to work it out. Plus I agreed to get married at her church if she would convert to Catholic. Worked out pretty well."

Nigel shook his head. He would never understand anyone who let religion get between them and the one they love. This was clearly a man he could get along with.

"So no fishy stories, theories, rumors that you can think of to help point me in the right direction?"

Clarence seemed to give it some real thought. Nigel noticed in the few minutes since he mentioned his job here in town, Clarence hadn't taken another drink of beer. He liked Clarence all the better for it.

His new friend shook his head, "No, I'm sorry. I can't think of anything."

"That's quite all right. Thanks for the beer. Maybe I'll come back by next time I'm in your neighborhood."

His face lit up. "Sure, that would be great."

He really did seem disappointed that he couldn't give any information, Nigel decided as he left the man's house. He just needed a lead, however slight it may seem to others, it could be just what he needed.

And as he walked down the driveway speckled with dried oil and cracked in chaotic patterns, he heard the voice of Clarence behind him. He turned and found his new friend coming toward him. “Hey, Mr. Baxter, I thought of something.”

“Please, Clarence, I’ve had your beer in the manliest part of your house, call me Nigel.”

He chuckled. “Sure, Nigel. Anyway, I’ve always heard stories around town about a place to partake in the less-than-legal activities.”

Nigel squinted at him. He couldn’t possibly mean…“You’re not referring to a speakeasy are you?”

“Yes, that’s it. A speakeasy. I don’t know where it is but the rumor, and again this is just a rumor, is that a guy by the name of Edward runs it. I can’t remember his last name. I’ve seen him around town a few times, but I’ve never talked to him myself, you know. He’s a strange little man.”

Nigel pulled the notebook from his inside pocket and rifled through the names of the people he had visited that day. No one named Edward was on it. Didn’t mean anything, not really. It also didn’t mean anything coming from the man he’d just met. Still, it could be promising. He jotted the name down.

“Thanks, Clarence. Call down to the station if you think of anything else.”

“Sure. And don’t forget I’ve got another beer in the cooler for you.”

Nigel strolled on down the street, a stranger named Edward running over and over in his mind. At the first payphone he found, he dropped his dime in and called the station. He needed to learn all he could about this new POI.

Chapter 22

Nigel

Nigel stepped up to his calendar with a pen in hand. It trembled slightly as he circled April 7. After getting an early morning call from the governor's office, he now knew he had a deadline. The day for the vote had been decided. He had less than two months to get the area cleaned up, and on a more personal level, to find out exactly what the hell was happening in this town.

A routine traffic stop resulted in the break Nigel needed. The only policeman employed in a tiny town out west happened to be on patrol when a truck rolled through going five over the posted speed limit. Normally, he could have let such things go, but the county sheriff had contacted him personally to let him know about the crack down on the alcohol trade.

Officer Remington Nash, named after the beloved gun company, told Nigel that he grew up in a house of two strict Baptist parents. "My father always taught me to pay attention to my intuition," he said with a fond smile. "He would say, 'It may seem womanly, son, but listen to your gut.' So that's what I did today."

Nigel didn't need to respond. It was as if living so far away from actual civilization had led to Nash needing just a little extra attention. Nonetheless, Nash finally did deliver the story.

"I flipped on the light as soon as I clocked him. He pulled over no problem, I called in the tags and made my way to the truck. All in all, it was really normal. When I got up to the driver's window, though, I thought he looked more corpse than any man had a right to look.

"'Evening, sir. Do you know why I pulled you over?' I asked.

"The driver's eyes darted to the mirror then to me. 'No idea, uh, sir. I'm just heading up the road a ways and plan on staying in a hotel somewhere. Probably going to find a diner before long and get myself a sandwich.'

"But the strong pull in my gut that my father had taught me so well to listen to once more demanded my attention. I slid my hand slowly to my holster. 'Would you mind stepping from the cab, sir?'

" 'Do we have to do that?' the man asked, a slight tremble sliding into his voice.

" 'Yes,' I said, 'Please step from the truck.'

"It's cold out here, as you know, and I swear I saw a drop of sweat roll down the side of the driver's face. I saw everything in that sweat, how this could play out. I waited with my heart booming in my chest. Then, he opened the door and slid out of the truck. After I searched it, I phoned to let you guys know what I found."

It turned out to be roughly a thousand dollars in illegal booze.

"You did really well, Officer Nash. I think you've earned a night on the town." Nigel glanced around. "Well, maybe not *this* town, but a town for sure."

Once Nigel got the driver back to town, he borrowed the chief's office as there was no interrogation room, a fact that Chief Ross most certainly resented. Nigel could use whatever room he wanted, sure, but using the chief's office became another way to remind Ross who had the power.

Nigel could smell the sweat and fear coming off the driver. It brought a sour stench to the office that would probably hang around the rest of the day.

"Thomas Mathews?" Nigel said, staring down at the driver's license in his hand. "Where were you heading before you got pulled over?" Nigel held the folder of the perp that contained everything he'd ever done in it, including being expelled from school in the third grade for lighting the trashcan on fire in the boy's bathroom. He'd only ever had minor run-ins with the law.

"I don't have to tell you anything." His words came out hoarse and directed at his feet.

"That is true, Mr. Mathews, however, I would advise spilling what you know. The governor of our great state has given me permission to put you away for twenty to thirty years for having that much illegal booze."

The number may have been an exaggeration, but Thomas didn't know that. The driver's face jerked like he'd just eaten garbage, but he remained silent.

Each moment of silence from the man was another moment closer to April 7. That was all Nigel could think of and it made him a bit frantic. "You know, in the olden days, one would undergo, let's call it torture, to get a confession. I can imagine that a great many people were willing to give up information when their fingernails were being crushed by screws or their arms were pulled from their sockets. I imagine that pain has a way of loosening the tongue. Would you like to find out?"

He didn't wait for an answer, but stood, walked around the desk and silently closed the door to the office. He stood directly behind Thomas. "I don't want to hurt you," he whispered, "but I don't want to *not* hurt you, you know? It always seems to do my soul some good to hurt people."

Before the driver could respond, his hand was in Nigel's. Nigel stared at the man as he lifted his eyes from their hands to his face. With their eyes locked, Nigel snapped the man's pinky, the breaking bone no louder than a baby bird snapping its neck.

The driver barely had time to react before Nigel's mouth was right next to his ear. "Now you listen to me, you worthless fuck. You will tell me something. You will tell me where you were taking the booze." He took a deep breath while Thomas whimpered next to him. "Give me a name."

Surprisingly, Thomas shook his head. Nigel responded by grabbing the already swelling pinky and twisting it a bit more. That brought such a noise forth from Thomas that someone came knocking on the chief's door. Nigel ignored it.

"Give me a name."

"I don't have a name." His voice came out as a wheeze full of tears.

"Then give me something." Nigel's words could barely be heard through his clenched teeth.

"I take the truck to an alley behind the Rialto. I park it and two days later, when I wake up, it's parked back at my house with cash in the driver's seat. Usually there are instructions on my next delivery." He broke off and clutched at his hand in pain. "I wish you hadn't broken my finger. I would've told you that."

Nigel leaned over so that his face was directly in front of Thomas. "If you don't want more pain, you better say something worth hearing."

The driver nodded a slow, steady nod. "I don't know who pays me or who takes the booze. But I do have a name." He hesitated a moment longer, but with a sigh he spilled it. "Terrance White."

The name meant nothing to Nigel Baxter who had fortunately spent a great deal of his life far from this place. "And what does Mr. Terrance White mean to me?"

Sweat continued to bead up all over Thomas' face. His left hand, the one with the broken pinky, shook in his right hand. "He makes, uh, hooch."

Nigel leaned back, a smile playing at his lips. "Does he?" The driver nodded. "Excellent. That's not great, but it's a start. If I can get a name out of him, I'll be that much closer, won't I?"

Chapter 23

Ezekiel

Ezekiel knew the name Thomas Mathews, but not because the man drove for him—Ezekiel let Johnny handle that side of the business—but from his butt being in the pew every Sunday morning, and more often than not, his weekly confessionals. Clearly his confessions were not entirely revealing as he'd never mentioned the extra-curricular activities he did with his company moving truck. Ironically, that part hurt Ezekiel more than he could have guessed it would.

"Has he ever done anything to make you doubt his devotion to his job?" Ezekiel asked. He held the cold glass of unsweet tea to his forehead, letting the condensation cool the skin.

"Boss, he does it for the money. I've never even met the man. One of my underlings recruited him because of the truck."

"Can we send someone in to kill him?"

"Now? Maybe tonight, but with that new inspector, I'm afraid it will be too late. They're likely already in an interview room." He shook his head, staring down at his black leather boots. "I don't know what to do."

In spite of this bad news, Ezekiel still had the scent of Mrs. Arrington hanging around his pores and it brought him relaxing joy. He wished that Johnny could handle this and go away. Still, Ezekiel had to give it his best focus. "Does this driver know anything that could…harm us?"

Wild Johnny gave this serious thought. His brow furrowed and he stared harder at his boots. "I can't say with any certainty that he does. He may know one of the moonshiners."

That caught Ezekiel off guard. Their moonshiners were among their most valuable assets, and they'd done a good job of keeping that information from public knowledge. "How would he know such information?"

"Well, I think he may be related to one."

"Surely he wouldn't roll over on his own relative, would he?"

"My guess is, given enough fear or pain, we'd roll over on anyone."

Ezekiel nodded. "Which one then?"

"Of the moonshiners? I do not know."

"Well, call them, each one. Let them know the law may be coming down on them." He sighed. "We need to find out who it is and maybe we can hide their stuff. If we have enough time, we can make this work."

After Wild Johnny left, Ezekiel sat in the living room of the house owned by the church. His thoughts left the work to Johnny so that he could return to the woman he'd spent the afternoon with. He felt consumed by her and not for the first time. Normally, he had an easier time of dealing with it, but here he was, swimming in the memory of her.

When he reached the bottom of his tea glass, he could no longer stand it. He grabbed the phone and he called the Arrington house, hoping to hear her voice again.

She answered on the third ring. “Hello?”

“Mrs. Arrington, I’ve been thinking about you.” A whirl of excitement tore through his belly like a sharp knife through thin skin.

For a moment, she didn’t answer. When she did, her voice revealed none of the excitement he had hoped for. “Why, hello, Brother Ezekiel. Yes, Robert is still planning on coming to your house on Sunday, I thank you for asking.”

“Clearly, you’re not alone, so I’ll make this brief: I want to see you again, and soon.”

“We’ll be praying for you, too, Brother Ezekiel.”

As he chuckled, he grazed the swelling in his pants, which responded pleasantly. “I’ll see you soon, Lucy, my dear. Take care of that boy of yours.”

“All right, you too. We’ll see you bright and early on Sunday morning.”

Ezekiel slid the phone back into its cradle and smiled. He’d catch hell for this later, the next time he saw Lucy, but for now he was content to have heard her voice. He hoped that the temporary relief would allow him to focus on his work again.

Chapter 24

Robert

Robert held his ridiculously heavy Algebra textbook on his lap and doodled in the margins of his homework while his mother spoke on the phone. He didn't notice the phone ring, but when she said "Brother Ezekiel," Robert tuned in to the rest of the conversation. While he couldn't hear the other side, it was clear that the preacher was calling with some type of prayer request.

But something bothered him about the phone call. He wrote Becky's name just to see what it looked like written out on his paper. Then it occurred to him: Why had the preacher spoken to his mom and not his dad?

It wasn't unheard of for Ezekiel to call and speak to his mom, but that was usually when his dad was out, working the fields or stuck in town. This was a whole new thing Robert had never experienced. So when his mom hung up the phone, he kept his eyes on her, trying to ascertain why the preacher wouldn't prefer his dad.

His first thought, and the one that would haunt Robert for a few nights, was that Ezekiel was calling to spill the secrets of their Sunday afternoon meetings. He'd been assured over and over again by Ezekiel that nothing would be said of what transpired in his house, but the fear still hung around him like tinsel on a dried out Christmas tree.

One thought rose into his mind, *He only said he wouldn't tell your* dad; *he never said anything about your mother.*

The thought made him visibly shake. He decided that he should watch his mother a little more closely whenever she was around Ezekiel. He simply didn't know what he would do if his mom found out about the secrets he told the preacher.

Chapter 25

Nigel

It was supposed to be a simple interview with a suspected moonshiner. Terrance White lived in a rundown house caked with the red dirt from the road in front. The front porch sagged to one side like a stroke victim's face and even in winter, it was clear the lawn hadn't been mowed since before the previous summer.

"This looks like paradise," Nigel said before he pulled himself out of the car. The officer who came with him, Doug Adams, nodded his agreement before getting out. Adams had gone to high school with Terrance, had actually been on the track team with him, and seemed to take it personally that his old running mate had turned to making illegal hooch. He'd insisted on coming with Nigel.

They mounted the porch the way one might mount a three-dollar whore after a busy night: with trepidation and a little disgust. With a quick glance at Officer Adams, Nigel rapped his knuckles against the unfinished, splintered front door of 318 Choctaw Road. "Mr. White? Mr. White, are you home?" he called out. The two policemen stood on the small stoop in silence, the beating of their hearts the loudest thing on that quiet back road.

Nigel turned to Adams. "What do you think?"

“Let’s take a peek in the back.”

Nigel nodded. “Lead the way, Officer.”

Adams stepped off the side of the porch and walked around the corner of the house. A fence, if so crude a structure could be called a fence, blocked the backyard from view of the men. It looked as if Terrance had taken every spare tree limb he could find and nailed them to a beam running parallel to the ground. “Hey, Terrence, you back here?” Adams reached the fence and stood on his tiptoes to peer over the top. An explosion distorted the quiet afternoon and tore a hole in the fence and Officer’s Adams’ midsection.

The young officer turned back toward Nigel just in time for the inspector to watch most of his blood pour out over his pants. Nigel kept his cool and didn’t run forward. Instead he reached into his jacket to pull his sidearm free. A face appeared in the new hole in the fence, presumably that of Terrance White. He had a manic smile on his face and a pistol in his hand that he aimed at Nigel.

Nigel fired his own gun twice, the second bullet finding the forehead of his assailant, while Terrance managed to fire once, grazing Nigel’s right arm, tearing cloth and flesh as it passed by.

Once he was sure the criminal was dead, Nigel rushed forward to find that Officer Adams was already gone, his eyes wide and confused, his hands holding the wound in his stomach like a newborn baby.

Nigel cursed the paperwork this would cause, but he knew for sure that there was at least one less moonshiner in his town, and that was enough to celebrate.

Chapter 26

Robert

Robert hadn't meant to spy on his mother, but his curiosity got the better of him. Ever since the night when the preacher had called to speak to her, he'd been determined to find out what was going on.

He got home from school and found his dad out working. "Hey, Dad, where's Mom?"

Mike paused from his work to look at his son. "Shouldn't you be doing homework instead of worrying over your mother?"

His dad always had to make comments like this. He never seemed to show his love for Robert but always wanted him to work. It was difficult on most days and probably seriously contributed to his rebellion. Still, Mike was his dad and Robert did his best to love him.

"I don't have any homework tonight," Robert responded. "I'm actually ahead."

"That right?" He nearly smiled. "Well, good. Your mother went into town, I think to buy some groceries. And she also mentioned stopping by the church to help print the bulletins for Sunday."

"OK, thanks, Dad. Can I take the truck into town to visit a couple of friends?"

Robert could tell his dad wanted him to work, needed the help. So he threw in, "I've got youth group tonight and I want to pick up a couple of the guys I've been praying for to go with me." He had no intention of doing any of that, of course, but mentioning prayer and church always worked on Mike.

"Sure, Son, take the truck." This time he did smile, and Robert felt the faint traces of guilt he'd once been so familiar with. He shrugged it off and went to the truck.

Once in town, he made his way to the church. He saw his mom's car in the parking lot. He pulled in next to her and threw the truck into neutral, kicked the parking brake, and jumped from the old beater. He looked at his parents' car then turned, not toward the church, but toward the preacher's house.

The gravel crunched under his shoes as he walked. He kept his eyes ahead, wondering what he was doing, what it was that he suspected. Something in his gut stirred and kept him walking. What if his mom was in there, alone, with the preacher? Maybe it was an entirely innocent interaction between them, but he couldn't be sure.

He went up to the corner of the house and gazed up to the front door, a door he'd gone through many times. Beside the door, taking up most of the front porch, was a large window. Robert could see the curtains were closed; they'd always been opened when he'd come. He tapped his finger against his leg and waited, a moment of indecision trembling through him.

At last he stepped up onto the porch and approached the door. But before he could push the doorbell, he heard his mother speak. "I do enjoy these afternoons. I sometimes wish it could be like this all the time." She laughed then, a sound unlike anything Robert had ever heard her make.

"Me too," Ezekiel said. "I think about it more than you know. We'd have to leave, but that would be worth it, wouldn't it?"

"We just have to wait until Robert graduates. I can't stand the thought of him alone with Mike. That man would tear our child apart if he could."

Robert held his hand up to the doorbell, the tremors jolting through it making it impossible to actually touch the button that would cause the doorbell to ring. His mom sounded *happy*, happier than he'd ever heard her. He couldn't interrupt that.

As he jogged back to the truck, the sound of the gravel loud in his ears, he wondered how long the affair had been going on. And the most important question, Should he tell anyone? He supposed he should, but a lot of lives were at stake in the telling. Could it be that he should keep even more secrets?

He climbed into the truck, wanting to put it all behind him and go see a certain Methodist girl who made him happy.

Chapter 27

Nigel

In the hours following the death of the moonshiner, the police tore the man's house apart. Not that there was much to tear apart, but they couldn't stop and mourn their fallen soldier, so they worked.

"I want any kind of address book, any name, anything we can use to keep moving forward with this." Nigel drank a cup of decaf coffee while they worked. He couldn't quite get the image out of his head of Officer Adams dying in front of him. It wasn't his first death, of course, but it never got easier to see.

"Sir?" Another young cop, this one barely out of high school, walked up to him holding a shipping label. "I found this attached to one of the boxes. The others look like they may have had them, but this was the only one still attached."

Nigel read the name and reread it. Edward Young. Wasn't that the name the old-timer drinking beer in his garage had told him? Edward, yes, that was it. "Thank you. You may have saved the day."

After phoning Mr. Edward Young, Nigel paid the man a visit. He was surprised to see how small the man was and how much his overly large mustache compensated for that. Still Edward seemed jovial enough when he answered the door.

"Mr. Young, thank you for seeing me." Nigel sat on a light blue couch facing Edward Young sitting on a replica, an expansive hardwood coffee table between them. Nigel leaned forward, toward the coffee table, while Edward leaned back, legs crossed at the knee, a knowing smirk on his face.

The outside of the house had not told the same tale as the inside. Approaching it, Nigel had thought it belonged to a middle-class, blue-collared family. The inside, however, spoke of wealth, the kind of money that almost became pointless to have.

"Of course, Inspector. I've heard a great deal about you in the few days since you came to town."

The small man wore a sweater vest with various colors waging a war against each other, with the only victim being the man wearing it. Under it he wore a pristine white button down shirt that looked like it had never even sat on a store shelf. Despite his tacky sweater, Edward Young had expensive taste, and apparently, the means to fulfill that taste. Nigel noted a tremor in Edward's hand as he drank coffee and the two made small talk. Nigel's own coffee sat on the table, forgotten and turning cold. He'd had enough for the day.

"Mr. Young, do you play poker?"

"Sir?"

"Poker. It's a bit of a card game. Usually involves money."

"I know the game."

"Have you ever played it?"

"I have not. Would you like to? I could get some cards."

"That's not necessary. I bring it up because you remind me of a time that I played poker with a friend of mine. He was deft at shuffling, even at keeping track of the cards. However, if he had a good hand, anyone in the room could tell it, and if you studied him enough, which I had, you could nearly tell exactly which cards he had. Last time we played, I cleaned him out, demanded he pay, and I never saw him again." Nigel shrugged. "He wasn't that good of a friend, anyway."

"I see."

"The reason I bring any of that up, Mr. Young, is because I would like to play you in poker."

"I just told you—"

"Yeah, yeah, you don't play. I got that." Nigel waved a hand, dismissing the idea. The cigarette in his fingers trailed smoke through the air. "What I mean is you couldn't hide a secret with a mug like that. You're easier to read than a *Dick and Jane* book."

Edward's face turned red, first with embarrassment, then with resentment. "If you're suggesting I'm hiding something from you—"

"Dammit, man," Nigel slammed his hand onto the top of the table, making the man and the coffee jump, "have you listened to anything I've said? I just told you, you're *not* hiding anything. You're attempting to conceal from me some truth, and it won't work. I can sit here all night arguing with you about it, but the fact is, you've got a secret, and you don't want to tell me about it."

"I…er…I don't know what you mean." His eyebrows furrowed on his large forehead where dots of sweat formed. His eyes darted toward the door.

Nigel smiled and stood. He casually walked to the door and stood in front of it. "Plan on leaving, Mr. Young, you'll have to go through me."

Edward let his eyes fall back to the table. He lifted

his coffee and took a sip, seemed to steal himself, and said, “Can you cut me a deal if I tell you?”

“Sure,” Nigel smiled, “anything you like.”

Edward gave an uncomfortable chuckle. “What I’d like most is to not be having this conversation.”

“Can’t do that, now can we?”

Edward shook his head as if this was a real question. He didn’t seem to have even heard it anyway. “What I want is to leave here, just pack up and leave town, never come back. If you give me two days, I’ll be out of here, and you will have a stack of names.”

“This better be some good information if I’m going to let you go.”

“It is. I’ll give you the location to the town’s only speakeasy, and you will let me go. After I’m gone, I will send a list of names to you, a list of the top booze smugglers in town and the name of the head man, the one behind it all.”

That caught Nigel’s attention. He stepped back to the couch and took his seat. “One man is behind it all?”

“Oh yes. All of Northwest Oklahoma is under his control. I’ve heard he’s killed a dozen men to keep his secret and to wipe out the competition.”

“What secret?”

“The secret of his identity. It’ll be quite the shocker.”

Nigel thought it over. “Give me all the names but his and you’ve got a deal.”

Edward shook his head. “I’m not a fool. You get the other guys, you could shake them down for the answers.”

“Okay then,” Nigel said with a smile. This was getting good. “One name. Not the top one. How about the bottom one? Who’s the least of those?”

Edward considered. “Yes, okay, I can do that. I have your word?”

“Sure.”

He sighed, a sound filled with mourning. He leaned forward and placed his coffee cup on the table, maybe the most coffee the coffee table had ever had on it. “The speakeasy is a place called the House out on the north side. There’s an abandoned building out there. I don’t know what it’s purpose once was, but now it is home to the hottest dance joint in this part of the country.”

Nigel pulled his small notebook from the inside pocket of his jacket. “And how do you know this? Are you a frequent visitor there?”

“Ha.” It was a sharp bark of a laugh. “My kind are not supported there. No, I’m the manager of the club. I handle all of the finances. And I own it.”

Nigel arched an eyebrow. “You’re the owner?”

“Yes.”

“And what do you mean by your kind?”

A small smile crossed Edward’s lips, almost invisible under his mustache. “I prefer the company of men.”

“Ah.” Nigel shifted in his chair uncomfortably. “So this club.” He cleared his throat. Edward smiled at his obvious discomfort. “When should I raid it?”

Edward leaned forward, placing his palms on the top of the table to either side of his coffee. “Give me two days. I can clear my name from the books, clear any evidence that I’ve been there. That will help keep your name clear.”

“And speaking of names, you owe me one.”

Edward sat back, a small sigh escaping his lips. “I do. And just as a show of good faith, I’ll tell you, he’s not the lowest on the totem pole. He's risen in the ranks from mere booze smuggler to being an all-around general assistant to the boss. He's an Australian by the name of Charles King."

Nigel jotted the name down. "And where could I find Mr. King?"

"I'm sure you could uncover that much. You are, after all, an inspector."

A flash of anger popped up on Nigel's face, but Nigel, a veteran poker player, concealed it before Edward could notice. "Good point, Mr. Young, very good point." He stuffed the small notebook back into the inner pocket of his jacket. "I will give you two days. Have all of your paperwork ready to go." He stood and offered a hand. "It was a pleasure working with you today, Mr. Young."

He walked out of the house, thinking back on the conversation. He would look into this Charles King, but he doubted that Mr. Young would call him and provide the rest of the names. Yes, after a brief deliberation fueled by the anger he felt, he decided Mr. King could wait, at least another day.

Chapter 28

Ezekiel

"Did I ever tell you why I started making booze?" Ezekiel rode in the passenger seat of the '56 Chevy that Wild Johnny drove. The streetlights overhead cast the interior of the car in alternating patterns of light and shadow as they drove the streets of their small town.

"No, boss, you haven't."

Ezekiel noticed that he didn't take his eyes from the road, but the toothpick in his teeth bounced with nervous excitement. Johnny had been around the business for a long time, but never really got the whole story.

The loss of product and the moonshiner, Terrence White, brought Ezekiel back to reality, forcing Lucy and the foolish notion of love out of his mind, at least for the time being. He could be thankful that Terrance went out with a fight, taking one officer with him, rather than being arrested and risking more names pouring into the inspector's ears.

Tonight he felt nostalgic for the past, the simpler times. He recounted for Johnny the financial woes of the church and the idea Mary had to start making illegal hooch to ensure the church could stay open. "It was Mary who ran the company in the beginning. She had a better sense for it. I tried to shut it down more than once, but she had a drive in her. She always enjoyed having her own thing that wasn't simply a ladies prayer meeting. It gave meaning to her life.

"When she died, well, you remember Mary, don't you?"

"Sure, boss." The toothpick jolted up and down with his words.

"When she died, my whole world changed. I no longer had the moral compass, and I couldn't keep focused on God. I keep preaching because it keeps me doing something, gives me an excuse to stay around this town, but some days, I'm not sure I want to even do that anymore." Johnny's eyes darted away from the road toward him. He'd surprised him; hell, he'd surprised himself. But the more he thought about leaving, packing it up with Lucy and heading out of town, he loved the idea. He had enough money to keep them comfortable for the rest of their lives.

They continued passing under streetlights, easing in and out of shadows at an innocuous pace. The preacher kept his eyes on the passing storefronts and houses.

"How do you keep people from knowing you're behind it all, the Baptist preacher?"

"There are rumors of course, but if I hear them, I squelch them. Not by denying them, but by embellishing them. Most people will not believe if the truth is told to them directly, but will believe if the accused maintains their innocence."

"Wise words."

"Ha. You should hear me when I'm sober."

The two drove on in silence, allowing the landscape of their town to guide them. They had no specific destination in mind, Ezekiel simply needed to be out, searching for the answer to what he must do next. He had an inkling, a terrifying truth that was slowly forming in his brain. "We're going to go to war, aren't we, Johnny?"

The lines of Johnny's face were thrown into deeper shadow as he discarded the toothpick and lit a cigarette, making him look much older. "It may very well be, boss."

Ezekiel nodded. "If we want to continue the comforts we are currently enjoying, we will have to fight for that. If alcohol is legal, where can we go from there?"

"I have a few ideas, boss, but why don't we wait until we need them before we talk about them?"

The preacher turned in his seat and peered at the man driving. He knew Johnny hoped to lead a criminal crew of his own, but he didn't think his right-hand man would leave the fold. He would have to keep a closer watch on him, but for now, he let the issue drop.

A stoplight turned red and Johnny brought the car to a stop. An old Ford truck pulled up next to them on the passenger side. Ezekiel glanced over and saw Charles King driving the truck, waving at him through the open window.

Ezekiel rolled the window down the rest of the way. "Charles, what's going on?"

"Hey, boss, I was talking to that lady who dates that guy from the club, you know?"

The preacher sucked in his breath and held it for a moment. This was the way that Charles usually spoke, using no names and general statements that don't give many clues as to what he's talking about. "Who are you talking about, Charles?"

He shook his head. "That doesn't matter. What matters is that little guy that runs the club?"

"Edward Young."

"Yeah, anyway that lady said her guy said that the club guy was going to split tonight, like leave town. So I thought you should know about it."

Ezekiel thanked him before Johnny drove away and the night took a much darker turn.

****

With Lucy added to the mix of Mary and Ezekiel, the money rained down like manna from Heaven. There were only a few holdouts left in town or people who didn't like Ezekiel's operation. Of course, no one knew it was him, but enough people suspected and enough rumors flew around the town that he really had to watch his steps.

Things took a new, interesting turn when a young kid, a punk who managed to get himself thrown out of school and had earned some community service time around the church. The kid went by Michael, and he was the exact kind of kid the team needed to run booze for them.

Mary was the one who spoke to him, first inviting him into their house for dinner, trying to befriend him.

"Have you ever attended church?" Mary asked him over dinner that night. Ezekiel passed the plate of rolls over to the young punk and eyed him warily. Mary's ideas so far had panned out just fine, but this one seemed to be the riskiest so far.

He gave a harsh laugh. "In this part of the world, have you ever met anyone who hasn't?"

"That's a fair point," she said with a smile. "But did you learn anything?"

"I learned that not everyone pays attention to what's said in the pulpit on Sunday mornings. And I don't much tolerate hypocrisy."

Mary took a bite, allowing the thought to settle over the table. Ezekiel kept his eyes on the kid at the end of the table, wondering if this could possibly work as well as her other ideas had worked. Nonetheless, Ezekiel trusted her to work things out.

Days later, Mary hired him, following the end of his community service, to do some odd jobs around the house and the church. Little by little, she earned his trust, and he earned hers. Ezekiel started having Michael run small deliveries for him, in sealed unmarked boxes, that he never asked questions about. While Michael may have been rude and arrogant, he also had a knack for understanding things, for finding answers to difficult puzzles.

Weeks went by in that manner, with young Michael working for them, earning a pretty good living for himself, and helping the church to thrive. Ezekiel felt that their business had grown to the perfect size. The church's financial woes had diminished to the point that Ezekiel could focus solely on preaching and Mary could handle all of the less legal sides of things.

Mary, however, wanted the business to continue to grow. "Ezekiel," she said one night just after their first year in town, "we could keep growing and never have to worry about money again."

Ezekiel shook his head. "The idea was to keep the church from closing. I think we've done that. We need to sock away enough to ensure it stays open, then we can think about closing it down."

"None of my friends have anything to do during the day. They cook, they clean, and they wait for their men to return home. I have something. And I don't know that I want to let it go."

The emotion coming off of his wife was like a strong Oklahoma wind, something that could not be ignored. He put a hand on her shoulder and smiled. "Okay, Mary, but you're in charge of it. Be careful."

She smiled and wrapped her arms around him.

For the next two years, Mary ran the business and held onto the reins in a closed-tight fist.

As Mary's bootlegging grew, she recruited more to work for her and began to undercut the prices of the competitors around the town. Ezekiel didn't know at the time just how ambitious his wife was. He found out much later, too late in fact, how far her hand stretched. He spoke in the pulpit about the dangers of greed, but she paid no attention to his warnings.

Chapter 29

Ezekiel

Ezekiel couldn't get any of it out of his head. Why would Edward Young try to leave? Was he attempting to steal from him?

"Why don't we stop by the House?" Ezekiel asked. Charles King drove one of Mike Arrington's work trucks off into the west, away from the trouble he'd caused with this information.

The House was an old building on the north side of town near the railroad tracks. Any businesses that once thrived in the area went defunct long ago. Since then, the biggest of the abandoned buildings had become a speakeasy of sorts, but only on the first floor. Other floors in the building weren't as safe with pieces of the floor missing and no electricity. He rarely went but he did provide all the booze and on most occasions, they had a hell of a jazz band that played.

Johnny turned in that direction and, in less than two minutes, they pulled into a parking spot downtown. An idling car set a block down, the driver reading a newspaper and smoking a clay pipe. Ezekiel and Johnny strolled up to it, and Johnny tapped on the window.

The driver rolled it down and said, "Yeah?"

"I'm here to meet a stranger."

The driver took a pull from his pipe and let the

smoke roll out of his mouth, the sweet smell of pipe tobacco wafting over them. “Get in.”

He drove the pair three blocks north to the building. From the outside no one could tell what was going on inside. That was the main reason for the driver. A lot of cars downtown didn’t seem out of place, but a lot of cars packed around an abandoned building did.

The two got out and approached the door. Johnny knocked and a piece of the door slid to the side. They could make out a pair of brown eyes surrounded by brown skin.

“I’m a stranger in a strange land,” Johnny recited the password for the club.

The slit closed and the door opened a few seconds later. Light and music poured out through the opening along with the smoke of a thousand cigarettes. “Welcome, gentlemen,” the doorman, a short, gruff man who worked on sanitation during the day, said.

Ezekiel and Johnny crossed the threshold and meandered down a hallway to another doorway. The music, though soft in the hallway, could be heard tremendously through the next door. Johnny opened it, and the loud jazz rolled over them. Fifty couples gyrated on the dance floor while at least another hundred different people hung around the edges. It was a thing of beauty to see everyone with a drink in their hands.

Tables lined the walls and lit candles decorated the middle of each table and hung on the walls. In the corner, a small stage had been built to provide the band a place to play. Carpets covered the walls to keep the music in the room. It was one of Ezekiel’s favorite places and he wished to God he owned it. Still it couldn’t stay open if it weren’t for the alcohol he provided.

On the wall opposite the stage was a wooden bar. The crowd of people trying to get to the bar were three deep and three different people tended the cramped area behind the bar. They looked exhausted yet happy. And of course they were happy: they were making lots of money.

A quick glance into the room was all that Ezekiel could afford. No matter how much he loved the music and sights of the people dancing and, more importantly, drinking, he could not afford for anyone to see him in this place. He was, after all, a preacher, and he was certain that his presence would kill the vibe out here. Johnny slid the door back into position and led the way past the room down a side hall to the back of the building where they found a thick mahogany door.

This door led to an office. Whatever the room housed in its former life, it was not an office. It could, in fact, fit five or six offices inside of it. In the center, sat a dark walnut desk surrounded by lit candles. Behind the desk, they found the small man they came to see. His bald head gleamed in the candlelight. He wore thick glasses on his face below which could be found his overly large mustache. He looked up when the two walked in and he dropped his hand back to his lap, groping for something under his desk.

"Let go of that shotgun, Eddie," Johnny said. He was one of the few people who got away with calling him Eddie. "We're not here to hurt you."

Ezekiel could see the struggle it took for the little man to take his hand away from the gun.

A forced smile surfaced on Edward's face. "Come in, come in." He stood and waved them over. Even with the candles and lanterns, shadows crept around the edges of the room. Ezekiel and Johnny eased into the two chairs in front of the desk. Edward sat back in his chair, pulled the stacks of money and notebooks he'd been going over off the desktop and slid it all into a drawer. "Welcome, gentlemen. I did not expect you or I would have had a car waiting for you. You could have taken the back entrance. It is more secluded."

"I appreciate that, Edward, however, I wanted the element of surprise."

The little man's eyes shot up behind his glasses. "Surprise? Well, I *am* surprised."

"What do you know about Inspector Nigel Baxter?"

"Nigel Baxter? That's an interesting name, isn't it?" His mustache quivered as he paused to wipe at his forehead. "I don't believe he's from around here." He shrugged his shoulders. "Are you sure you have the name right?"

Ezekiel made an excellent attempt at hiding his anger. "Cut the crap, Edward. I will pull my booze outta this place in a second."

"You wouldn't." Surprisingly, he managed to say it without a tremor in his voice. "You make too much money here."

"You're right." Ezekiel turned to Johnny. "Shoot him."

Johnny nodded, stood, and pulled his side piece in one fluid motion. It was a .357 Magnum that would tear the mustache off, along with most of his face. Johnny allowed the barrel to just touch the skin on Edward's forehead when Edward said, "Nigel Baxter, did you say? That name does sound familiar now that you mention it."

Johnny smiled and returned to his seat, but kept his gun in his hands.

"Nigel Baxter came up here from Oklahoma City. Before that, he worked in Chicago during the national prohibition. He brought down some tough crime syndicates and now he's here. Honestly, Ezekiel, if I were you, I would cut and run. It's not worth hanging around here for this."

Ezekiel sat back and took a breath. "Can we stop him?"

"Stop him? Did you not hear what I said about him? I'm cleaning out. Tonight is the last night of the House. I'm taking my cash and getting out of town."

As he said this, his voice became shakier and more manic. His eyes, magnified by the thick lenses, darted back and forth between the two men sitting across from him. He dabbed some sweat on his gleaming forehead once more.

Silence fell over the room like shadows. Ezekiel let his eyes wander as he pondered what the man had said. There was no one else here. Where Edward usually had a guard standing, there stood a suitcase packed full. Normal things that decorated the walls were missing.

"You're serious?" Ezekiel asked. "You are planning on leaving?" He kept his voice soft, full of concern, masking the anger he truly felt.

"What choice do I have? As soon as I learned Nigel Baxter would be investigating the alcohol situation in this town, I made plans to get out. It's only a matter of time before he discovers me."

Ezekiel leaned forward and put his elbows on the desk. In a quiet voice he said, "And when did you plan to tell me?"

"Ezekiel, you're busy, and I didn't want to weigh down your schedule with this."

Several things happened following this comment. Ezekiel jumped to his feet, pulling a blade from the inside pocket of his suit in the process, Edward grabbed for the shotgun attached to the bottom of his desk, Johnny grabbed Ezekiel to pull him out of the way, and the door to the office burst open with someone shouting, "Cops!"

Edward pulled the trigger on his gun, a gun that he had never fired before. He was shocked to find that he'd never even bothered loading it. Ezekiel hit the floor, the knife flying from his hand. Johnny took a look down at his fallen boss and turned toward the retreating Edward. Johnny chased after him and before Ezekiel could stand, had caught him and laid a powerful fist against the side of his face, his glasses shattering on the concrete floor beside him.

Ezekiel could hear a cacophony coming from the dance hall. The music cut, people screamed, and cops shouted.

"What do we do, boss?"

Ezekiel threw another look back at the office door where the stranger had just come through. "That man may have been our savior. Let's get outta here."

"What about him?" Edward moaned at Johnny's feet, holding his face.

Ezekiel held out his hand for Johnny's gun which he handed over. Racing footsteps could be heard pounding down the hallway outside of the office, so Johnny didn't give his boss the chance to fire the weapon. Without a moment's hesitation, he grabbed Ezekiel's arm and pulled him into the shadows toward the backdoor. They got out of the building and ran.

Chapter 30

Robert

Robert had finally impressed Charles with the amount of booze that he could now handle. Unfortunately for Robert, the increased amount of alcohol in his life began to have a negative effect. His grades slipped and his chores were only half done most days. This brought him under the gazing scrutiny of his father, Mike.

Mike often proclaimed loudly that Robert would be forcefully removed from the house the day after he graduated high school and it was expected for the boy to become successful in whatever he decided to do. College wasn't really spoken of in the Arrington house, but Robert did plan on at least applying. He had his own hopes to not be a farmer besides his father expecting, rather loudly, that he run the family farm one day.

A fist boomed into Robert's door which opened before he had a chance to say anything. The knock brought Robert out of his sleep. He remembered sitting down at his desk to work on homework, but the words had blurred and his eyes had failed. Sleep was always easier than homework.

"What's going on?" Robert bleary said as Mike grabbed his shoulder.

"Robert, you've been sleeping. Shouldn't you be

studying?"

Robert glanced down at the books. He had one, his Literature book, opened to a short story he should have read yesterday. He had a quiz over it and another story tomorrow. On top of that, he'd fallen behind on his math homework. He'd been quite drunk, so none of it was really making much sense.

"Yeah, thanks, Dad. I'm really tired." He didn't turn his head toward his father for fear the smell would reveal his afternoon revelries.

"I would have guessed as much. Robert, I don't know what's going on with you. Brother Ezekiel assures me you're doing great, that your weekly meetings have been enough to assure him that you're heading down the right path, but I'm starting to feel like things have changed somehow. I like to think I'm an observant father and I can't pretend that this didn't all start with that damned Fall Festival." His hand still clutched Robert's shoulder and squeezed it harder than necessary.

This helped sober Robert up more than the sleep; he'd only heard his father cuss once so that, along with the pain in his shoulder, woke him right up.

"It started then because of a girl," Mike continued. "You don't tell your mother and me anything, but it's clear you're still dating her despite the rigorous schedule we keep for you." He sighed. "Brother Ezekiel has spoken highly of her family, though they are not Baptists. So we think it's time you bring her around for dinner. Your mother would like to meet her."

Robert jumped as if his dad had squeezed his shoulder again. "Really? When do you want her to come?"

"Tonight, if at all possible. I want you to call her and

find out, then go get her if she can come."

"Yes, sir. I'll do it."

Mike kept his gaze on his son, trying, so it seemed to Robert, to see beyond the surface. Robert kept his eyes on his dad's, but found it difficult to focus them. The alcohol still played with his senses, making it difficult to focus on anything. His stomach roiled and he felt the need to puke. It was a feeling he'd gotten used to over the last few days. Still, his heart hammered at the idea of bringing Becky to his house to meet his parents. Finally his dad left the room, but refused to close the door on his way out.

Robert stood, holding onto the chair to keep himself steady. He shook his head, hoping to clear it, and nearly fell over. He wished the sleep had taken away more of the effects of the alcohol. He grabbed the phone in the living room, the one he'd so recently watched his mother answer and speak with the preacher. He got through to the operator and she connected him to Becky.

The next thing he remembered for sure, he was sitting in the driver's seat of his dad's truck heading to Becky's to pick up his girl for a date with his parents. He wasn't sure what to make of the predicament. He'd really believed he could just continue on until he graduated in May, then maybe he and Becky could go to college or maybe just somewhere far from home, far from the rigors of farm life.

He focused on the road, or attempted to; the yellow line marking the center slid left and right with each blink of his eyes. Still, he managed to keep the tires on the path to Becky's, but he kept getting distracted, thinking about what she would say to his parents. He was nervous. He found that he wanted them to like her. He wanted them to see her the way that he saw her.

The right front tire found the edge of the road and pulled the truck that way. Robert corrected it easily, once more focusing on that dancing yellow line in the center of the highway.

The line made him think of Becky's yellow dress, the one she'd been wearing the last time they'd made love. He thought of the way that dress had looked in the moonlight, crumpled on the seat next to him as she straddled his legs, her hair tickling his chest and shoulders as they kissed. Whatever happened with his parents tonight, he knew he'd never let that go.

Again, the tire pulled the truck off the road. This time Robert's reactions were a little slower, like he was moving through syrup, the nerves in his limbs not quite getting the message as fast as they should have. Almost the entire truck went off the road before he got it under control again. He let his foot off the gas, slowing the truck and watching the road coming. It began to split into two parts. He blinked again, downshifted. The road merged back into one piece, and he once more pushed down on the gas, shifting back up. He let his foot determine the speed.

He could see the lights of town up ahead. He thought of seeing those lights from a different angle with a naked Becky sitting on the bench seat beside him. Once they'd sat side by side and enjoyed the comfort they felt with each other while naked. They didn't make love that time, only watched the city with nothing between them. That was the moment he knew he loved her more than he would love anyone. That electric touch between them.

Those city lights blurred and slid to the right then flipped entirely upside down. The truck had left the road again, this time without Robert noticing, not until it was too late. He jerked at the wheel and the momentum of the truck threw it, first on its side, then onto the roof. Robert, not wearing a seatbelt, fell onto the hard metal surface of the top of the truck, broken glass spraying all around him. His eyes focused on those city lights in the distance before they blurred again, then everything went dark.

Chapter 31

Ezekiel

"I think you need to leave town for a little while, boss."

Ezekiel didn't say anything. He knew that Johnny meant well, but he also knew that he'd just been through the closest call of his life and he wasn't out of it yet. He lay on the floorboard in the backseat of the loner Ford Johnny now drove. It wasn't the most comfortable ride, but Ezekiel suspected it was more comfortable than the jail cells downtown. He'd been there to care for his sheep and take care of his business. But never as a criminal.

When they busted out of the back door of the House, they had used the cover of darkness to aid their escape. Since no one knew about the backdoor, it was unguarded. It was clear that Baxter had elicited the help of the surrounding towns and counties as police cars and officers were everywhere, way more than the little town had ever seen. Johnny managed to work his way through the shadows away from the cop cars. He couldn't risk getting to his own car. But a garage just a block away from the House held the loner sedan. While Johnny got it, Ezekiel worked his way north of the House. Nothing could be seen out there past the railroad tracks. He waited in the relative safety of a wheat field for the excitement to die down enough for Johnny to come and get him.

More blue and red lights flashed through the inside of the car. Ezekiel tried to bury himself deeper into the floorboard, sure that this one would be after them, but the lights disappeared a moment later. He relaxed his hand that gripped the blanket too tightly. He did not want to get caught, but he especially did not want to get caught like this: hiding on his belly in the backseat of a car.

"How did the heat find out about the House?"

Again Johnny spoke to Ezekiel who wasn't speaking back. But this was a question Ezekiel had already run through his head several times. He could come up with no answer except one, and Johnny voiced it before he had the chance.

"Think someone ratted us out?"

It was precisely what Ezekiel was thinking. He remembered the way Edward had been packing up the cash and books. He dismissed the idea of Edward being the one, but his gut clenched at the thought of the strange, small man. He was the only logical traitor that Ezekiel could come to. Edward was getting everything and getting out because he knew the cops would be busting the place any day. He obviously didn't expect it to happen so soon.

From the floorboard, Ezekiel said, "We have to find that damned Edward Young. A moment more and he'd already be dead."

"Sorry about that, boss. Better he get arrested than you."

"I'll never blame you or your sharp ears for getting us out of there. They had to have arrested him, right? Can we get in? Did Baxter get rid of all the cops on our payroll?"

In lieu of an answer, the car came to a stop and Johnny got out. Before closing the door he said, "I'll check with Benny."

Ezekiel smiled and thought of Benny. He'd nearly forgotten about the overweight, alcoholic janitor who cleaned the police station. The man was close to retirement and knew he would never be able to afford it, so he took handouts from Ezekiel and his ilk for information and for the rare meeting inside the jail. Ezekiel had only had to do that twice, once for a customer who owed him a great deal of money, the second for an employee who had managed to get caught with a great deal of booze. He held a meeting with them, not to kill them, but to warn them that death would find them if they didn't do a few things for him. Half of them could still be counted among the living.

Johnny climbed back in the car and shivered. A fine layer of ice coated his back. Ezekiel watched it gleam in the streetlight. "Benny's there. So's Edward. He said we wait two hours, he can get us in. He's got to get rid of the Inspector before he can. Place sounded like it was hopping tonight."

"Think we're safe to go home?"

Johnny shrugged. "I don't think anyone saw us. If they had we'd be caught already. My place is probably the least safe. At least you've got that hidden room so that if anyone manages to locate us, we can hide in there."

"That's good thinking. Head that way."

The next two hours were quiet, thankfully because the meeting with Edward would change everything for Ezekiel and the town he called home.

Chapter 32

Nigel

"You told me two days. Two days!" Edward Young sobbed, snot ran freely into his mustache, and his cheeks burned red. It was a sight that Nigel could hardly stand. With bars between them, Nigel at least felt distanced from the strange little man. Still, Nigel had lied to him and felt he must try to explain.

"I didn't believe you." Nigel responded. "Maybe you shouldn't have believed me."

"Maybe? It's quite obvious I shouldn't have!" He sucked some snot down his throat. "Why would I have lied to you?"

"Why wouldn't you? If I let you go, what would possibly keep you from not giving me the information you promised?"

"You couldn't have put out a warrant for my arrest?"

"Yes, and waited years for that to do any good. No, I think this was the best method. Why don't you go ahead and tell me the names you were going to before all this? Then we'll see about getting you out of here."

"No, I won't. I'm not telling you anything. I could have been killed tonight because you came to talk to me. I can't say anything else."

"You could have been killed?" He arched his eyebrows. "Tonight? Before we got there, you mean?"

"Of course before you got there."

Nigel studied the strange man for a few moments more and thought. Surely, he decided, if someone had come to kill Edward, their car had to still be downtown. He decided to have someone look into it and turned to leave. Before he did, however, he said, "I'll have those names from you, Mr. Young. You can sit here for a few days, but we will find ways to get the information from you."

Edward said nothing to that, but leaned over and wept into his hands. Nigel watched him, wondering what he hoped to accomplish by crying like that. It didn't matter, he supposed. Nigel waited for a moment, next to the cell, the only sound in the room was Edward's sobs. Nigel didn't have time to wait for the queer to build up some gumption to talk to him. He blinked his eyes and had a difficult time opening them back up. He decided he was done.

He went down the short hallway of jail cells of the county jail. He opened the door at the end and found an officer standing guard. "I'm done with him. I'll try again tomorrow."

The weariness in Nigel built to a climax and he found himself thinking longingly of his bed. He did not wait for an answer from the officer but merely walked on toward the building's exit.

He passed the night janitor. "Have a good evening, Benny."

Benny smiled, always showing his full set of teeth when he did. "You, too, sir."

Nigel continued on. It had been a big day, full of big rewards. The governor should be quite happy with his results today. He would get more information out of

Edward Young and more arrests would be made. He smiled. He could be back in his own bed with his wife by the end of the week.

Of course, he had no idea that Edward Young would be dead by dawn.

Chapter 33

Robert

The young, brown haired woman introduced herself as Rhonda. She smiled a lot and kept asking questions concerning his needs, his comfort. She genuinely seemed interested in his well-being. “I am glad to see you’re awake. It took a while to figure out who you were. But I am happy to say that your parents are on their way.”

Parents? He wondered why his parents might be coming. Coming where? That was a good question, where was he?

Every surface looked white. In the background, he heard high-pitched beeping and a tube stuck out of his arm, connected to a bag of clear liquid. He attempted to get his bearings and couldn’t quite do it. He simply could not remember where he was or why he was here.

“Robert, are you feeling okay?” Rhonda was there again, forcing him to meet her eyes.

He moved his tongue in his mouth, wanting to speak and finding the words missing. He opened his mouth and sounds came out. They sounded similar to “I’m okay.”

She smiled and held up a glass of water with a bendy straw. He eagerly drank from it. The cool feeling slid down the inside of his body. It amazed him how it eased his pain like some miracle elixir. Still the effort of sitting up brought a pounding to his head that matched the background beeping. He also realized his right arm hurt worse than his head. He decided to attempt speaking again. "Where am I?"

Rhonda smiled, continued smiling, never stopped smiling. He wondered what her face might look like without a smile. "Well, you're in the hospital, sweetie." She let that sink in, and it did. He decided that the beeping and the tubes made sense in that context, but the reason didn't. The nurse continued, "A concerned citizen found your truck rolled over in a ditch just northwest of town. I'm afraid you've broken your arm."

That sparked some memories. Still it came with blurred edges and some gaps, but he did remember driving the truck. "How long have I been here?"

The nurse checked her watch. "I'd say about three hours. We didn't know who you were, couldn't find a wallet. The police finally found the registration in the truck. That helped us figure you out. Your parents were quite worried. They've been calling all the neighbors' houses. Anyway, they are coming here, eager to see you."

Robert nodded and took another sip of water. "My head hurts." Despite the water, his voice still sounded like the exhaust on his dad's work truck. It rumbled deep in his throat, felt almost like he swallowed part of the truck's windshield.

"I imagine it does." She checked his IV to ensure his inflow of fluids. "You hit your head pretty hard when you rolled the truck, one of the reasons we recommend you wear a seatbelt when you drive. Also your blood alcohol level was quite high."

She added this last as if she didn't want to say it, letting the smile, at last, slip from her face, and after she said it, Robert realized he didn't want to hear it. His heart rate jumped up and his breathing became more difficult. "Do you mean…?"

"You were quite drunk when you wrecked, yes. I'm not sure what will happen to you legally, but I can tell you that we'll get your head and arm taken care of. You may feel bad for a while, but I imagine a broken arm will be nothing compared to what you'll face when you leave here. I've known your dad from church."

She left him then, alone with his thoughts. He was in deep, of that he was sure, but he knew he couldn't say anything about Brother Ezekiel or Charles. Those were secrets he would have to keep as long as possible.

There was a light knock on the door and his parents entered the room. On his mother's face he saw only compassion and worry; on his father's, he saw that the old man already knew. One glance at that man's face and he wished that the rollover had killed him.

Chapter 34

Ezekiel

"Edward Young, I'm here to pray for your everlasting soul."

Edward lay on the smelly, thin cot in his cell, clearly unable to sleep. His head jerked up at the sound of Ezekiel's voice. Once, Ezekiel had opened his pantry to find a mouse eating some chocolate and staring back at him with naked horror. Here, he saw the same fear in the man who'd, up until recently, worked for him. It was that fear that stirred Ezekiel onward. Killing was a necessary part of the job, but seeing the fear on this man's face reminded Ezekiel of the power he felt.

"You see, the preacher of the First Baptist Church has no problem getting into the jail to pray for the incarcerated. Lining the pockets of those ignored by society certainly helps."

Edward stared in dumb silence, his eyes wide, nearly entirely black with his expanding pupil. He lifted a shaking hand to his temple, rubbing it absentmindedly.

"I need to know who ratted us out." Ezekiel stepped forward, grasping the bars of Edward's cage. "You must've suspected I would come along asking."

Edward nodded, his Adam's apple jumping up and down in his throat. The long hairs of his mustache danced with each exhalation of his breath. At last he whispered, "Will you kill me?"

Ezekiel chuckled, a chilling response to such a question. "If you're lucky. You didn't come to me. You didn't tell me what you knew. It was only because of those loyal to me that I was able to get there in time to find you. And it was mere luck that I escaped the House and didn't join you here.

"There's only one logical conclusion to your behavior. You *knew*, knew they were coming. So, how did you know? Who told you to expect an invasion? Who was it?"

"A name? You want a name?"

Ezekiel leaned into the bars. "Yes." His voice soft as down.

To Ezekiel's surprise, Edward smiled. "You really don't know, do you? You've remained so distant from your operation to make sure only a handful would know your true identity. You've had no idea the *cracks* that are forming in your empire. And now this Inspector is poking those cracks. This will all fall around you. And losing your preaching gig will be the last thing you need to worry about."

That cold dread that Ezekiel had been feeling all day doubled up in his gut, clenched at his balls, turning them this way and that. He felt he could vomit one second, and let loose his bowels the next. He kept his grip on the bars strong so that he wouldn't show the trembling that wracked his limbs. "Who told the cops about the House?" The softness went from his voice, his words came out harder than marble, heavier than lead.

The small man didn't seem to notice the change in tone, the threat of malice. He continued to smile. "It was me, *Brother* Ezekiel. I told Inspector Nigel Baxter. He gave me a window to get out and betrayed me. He was supposed to come two days from now. I wasn't supposed to be there. And neither were you. That's why I was packing. I spilled the secret."

Ezekiel stepped back from the bars, a rage he'd always felt below the surface since the death of Mary boiled up and erupted in a ball of fury. With hands that trembled from the anger and the fear and the betrayal, he pulled a key ring from his pocket. Edward saw the keys, and the smile promptly left his face, as if he'd been slapped.

"What's that you've got there?" Edward asked, his voice shaking worse than Ezekiel's hands.

"I told you it helped to line the pockets of those ignored by society. Benny will never have to work here again. In fact, he's found a nice secluded place to live out the rest of his days, enjoying a retirement none of us will know."

The panic that Ezekiel had watched unfold on Edward's face when he first spoke to him came back with a vengeance. It tore apart the normally good-humored face of the small man. As Ezekiel slipped the key into the cell, he also pulled a blade from his pocket that glinted in the light of the hallway. Edward apparently saw his only opportunity and rushed the bars. But just before he reached the door to the cell, Ezekiel threw it open and slipped the blade easily between Edward's ribs. Ezekiel imagined he heard the small man's lung pop; blood burst up through his throat and spilled out of his mouth.

"Dear Lord," said Ezekiel, the murderer and most renowned preacher in Northwest Oklahoma, "please deliver the soul of this sinner to the farthest depths of

Hell." He twisted the knife, widening the wound, bringing more warm, sticky blood spilling over his hand. "Give him no rest as his body rots in the ground." He pulled the knife, a spurt of blood following the removal of the blade. "And all God's people said, 'Amen.' " Edward dropped to the floor of his cell where he coughed and caught a few last breaths.

Ezekiel stood over him, pulling a white handkerchief from his pocket and cleaning the blade with it. He waited for the last breath, watching the man die but taking no pleasure in it. He felt his grip on the town loosening, his love for money blinding him. If he could no longer count on the House and his men were being taken out one by one, what would he do to make money? How would he feed his wolves like Wild Johnny?

Watching the man die, Ezekiel began to formulate a plan for retirement, one where he could convince Lucy to leave her husband, where they could leave, run away and find a regular life full of love and mirth. But he also thought it could be too late, it very well could be too late.

Chapter 35

Nigel

Nigel still couldn't comprehend what had happened. How had his prisoner been killed in his cell? All thought of finding a mysterious car in the parking lot left his mind as he grabbed the stack of papers and books on the desk nearest him and threw them. He roared in fury. He wanted to stick a knife in the men working last night who should have protected him.

He turned to the chief. "Is he in there?"

The chief nodded, casting a glance at the fallen papers. "You've got five minutes with him."

Nigel entered the chief's office. Officer Bob Daniels sat at the table. He wasn't cuffed but he looked like a wreck. His wrinkled shirt wasn't tucked in and his hair would probably never lay flat again.

Nigel sat across from him. He hid his fury as he asked, "Who visited the jail last night?"

"No one." The cop's voice quivered. "I swear."

"If no one visited the jail then that means you killed him."

"I didn't, I swear I didn't." He started to sob. "What about the janitor? Have you talked to him?"

"Benny? We haven't spoken to him yet. It was my understanding that with an officer on duty, we wouldn't need to speak to a janitor."

"I'm just saying that I didn't see him last night after two or three. He probably killed him and bolted."

Nigel glanced down at his notes. "And when did you discover the body of Mr. Edward Young?"

The cop hung his head. "Around six this morning, just before I was scheduled to leave for the day."

"So you think the man was murdered three or four hours before you discovered his body? And where were you all that time?"

Officer Daniels licked his lips and took a few breaths before answering. "I was asleep, sir."

"Asleep? Really? Do you think maybe that's why you didn't see Benny? It's hard to see someone when you have your eyes closed, isn't it?"

Inspector Baxter stood, stepped around the desk, and punched Officer Daniels square in the face. The hard meatpacking sound thudded in the walls of the small office. Nigel shook his hand to clear away the pain.

"I have a dead prisoner thanks to your negligence. I was going to be home before the week ended, but now I have to drag this out even longer. If you want to keep a job here, you say nothing about what I just did, and you start thinking of ways we can stop these murdering bootleggers."

He stormed out of the room without a further word. The chief eyed him suspiciously from the floor where he was piling the fallen papers. The sound of Nigel hitting the officer may have been louder than he originally thought. "I suppose he won't be any help after all. I think I'll finish my investigation elsewhere." Nigel went out into the bright sunlight.

At the very least, the murder of Edward Young confirmed Nigel's suspicions about someone controlling the booze in this part of the state. He wouldn't have believed it before coming here. He thought there might be a few booze runners and moonshiners, but a legitimate crime syndicate? Never. At least he now knew he was on the right track and making someone very uncomfortable.

Still, it gave him something to think about. And he had a name. Edward Young had delivered that much. Charles King. Nigel wouldn't go for him right away but would watch him. There was a chance he might see the crime boss before arresting this farmhand. Or at the very least, someone higher up. This was how he'd done things in Chicago and he would do them that way here.

He headed south, away from the station.

Nigel watched a not-unattractive but tired looking woman stride up to him on the sidewalk. "Are you the new inspector?"

"I see that my reputation is beginning to spread around this small town," he said with little more than a glance her way. Rage still bounced through his soul.

"Everything spreads around this town. My name is Lucy. I'm a…concerned citizen. As I understand it, you're trying to enforce that tired old law of prohibition."

"That is my job. Do you have some opinions about it?" He stopped moving to look into her eyes as they spoke.

"I think it is a silly law, no matter what the preacher says."

"And what preacher would that be?"

"Ezekiel Wilson." When she said the name, her voice took on a different tone, a note or two higher, and her face flushed lightly. Nigel decided not to comment on the change.

"He keeps coming up in conversation. I've met Mr.

Wilson and attended church there a time or two. I enjoyed talking with him, but I must say, his passion for prohibition is at least triple my own."

"So you don't want to enforce prohibition?"

"That is why I'm here, but I don't really care. Between you and me, I'm only enforcing it to help our chances of ending it. It's an idea from the governor himself and I think it a mighty good one. I had just hoped to get this region under control so I could head home."

She didn't say anything, just studied his face. "Did you have something more pressing you wanted to talk to me about?" he asked her.

"The people who were arrested last night, at the club, what will be happening to them?"

He arched an eyebrow. "How do you know about that?"

She shrugged. "Like I said, everything spreads around this town. Think of rumors as butter and the town a warm piece of toast." She giggled at her own analogy. "I was at the hospital last night with my son. He had an accident. I heard about it from one of the nurses who was glad she had to work."

"I see. Well, we had to transport most of them out of here to different counties as we don't have room for that many. Plus we had a special prisoner that I kept separated from the others."

"Oh, that little queer man? Does he really like men?"

Nigel was overcome with anger and frustration at this point. She threw out statements as if they were facts so nonchalantly. Of course, they were facts which was probably what caused the anger. "Listen, lady, if you just want gossip, you'll have to find yourself a salon or some other group of women to talk with you. I have things to attend to on this busiest of days."

She held up her hands. "I didn't mean to anger you. I just wanted to know if Brother Ezekiel was among those arrested last night, that's all. I went by his house when I heard about it early this morning, but he wasn't home."

This time Nigel didn't know what to say. Mr. Wilson's name had come up again and this time in such a strange fashion. "Why would the Baptist preacher have been in such a place? And why were you concerned enough to go by his house during the early hours of the morning?"

"I believe he goes there from time to time." She could not meet his eye, he noticed. "He searches for sinners. He is driven to find those most afflicted by the disease, as he calls it. He prays over people there and makes them feel uncomfortable. He really is a saint." Her cheeks turned red as she spoke of him. Just the thought of him seemed to electrify her senses. It was clear to Nigel that this Lucy might be in love with her preacher.

"You think he was there last night?" He pulled a small notepad from his pocket and jotted a few notes from the conversation.

"That's not a crime, is it? Because I don't believe Ezekiel is guilty of any crimes. I believe he is the man he claims to be. Why, every time I have ever seen him, he's been nothing short of the evangelist I see in the pulpit."

Nigel paused in his notetaking and stared into her eyes. "My, you have gotten defensive. Seem to be laying it on pretty thick, don't you?"

"Defensive?" She thought about it. "Well, if I have, it's your fault. With your questions I can't possibly answer." Her face turned surprisingly redder and her voice rose in volume. "Just forget I ever spoke to you, will you?" She turned to go.

He smiled. "Ma'am, I don't think I'll be able to do that. In fact, you've given me quite a lot to ponder over. Could you tell me your last name, Miss Lucy?"

She opened her mouth. Closed it. Opened it again, then turned and walked away. A genuine smile, the first he'd had since finding out about Edward Young, crossed his face. He liked her, and it certainly didn't take a genius to realize that she was deeply in love with Ezekiel Wilson. He wondered who she was, what her interest in the preacher was, and why she would immediately assume he'd been arrested last night. Surely that would have been bigger gossip than the arrest of a little gay man. Surely, he thought, and I need to see a preacher about my sins.

Chapter 36

Ezekiel

Saturday afternoons were usually reserved for finalizing the notes of his sermon for the next day, but today, Ezekiel found he couldn't quite focus his eyes on the notes he'd made. His Bible lay open in front of him, some passage from the Old Testament blurred with his smeared handwriting in the margins. He wanted sleep, he wanted to forget everything from the night before, he wanted to be done with everything, free from this life he'd chosen. Maybe he could find a way or maybe a way would be found for him. He wasn't sure.

In the next few months, he believed he would find that freedom, that he would be able to run away from this town, from this perceived profession, and find love and happiness at long last with Lucy.

When the phone rang, interrupting his thoughts, he sprinted across the room, toppling his chair in the process, and made it to his kitchen in record time. He clutched at the receiver, his knuckles turning white with the hope it gripped. He was disappointed to hear Mike's voice instead of Lucy's.

Ezekiel couldn't tell what emotions brewed in Mike's system that day. In fact, he seemed more devoid of feeling than anything else. Ezekiel, who knew the man probably better than Lucy did, had seen him cry and scream and curse the devil. He had never heard him like this. That brought Ezekiel out of his house when he should have been focusing on his sermon notes or trying to figure out what to do about the House, or conversing with Wild Johnny about any new prospects he might have. In his car, he thought of that damned Robert and what the kid had been doing the night before.

The hospital was its normal bustling self. The nurse, Rhonda, smiled when he came through the doors. "Hello, Brother Ezekiel. Here to see the Arringtons?" she asked.

"Yes, ma'am." He didn't typically wear a hat, he always wanted his hair to be pristine, but the morning had brought with it a new, and hopefully the last, cold front and the dying fight of a mild winter. Now he pulled the hat from his head and brushed at his hair with his fingertips. He followed Rhonda.

"Did Mr. Arrington say anything on the phone about Robert's accident?"

"He said Bobby had rolled the truck. That's all he told me."

She nodded as if she expected as much from Mr. Arrington. "Well, I won't say anything to you about it then, but just know, Robert is in big trouble. Hopefully you can help patch some of the mess he's made."

The hospital room was bright but not cheery. Mike sat in a corner, purposefully staring at the floor. Lucy sat beside her son, holding the hand not broken. She appeared shocked when the preacher walked in, but there was something else there, Ezekiel thought, like she couldn't quite believe he was real. Robert stared at the ceiling from his bed. He looked for all the world like he might be enjoying himself.

"Brother Ezekiel." The breathless voice of Lucy

came to him first. Ezekiel knew his purpose here, but the sight of her, looking so afraid and frail, made him want to comfort her, to take her out of here and away from the pain in this room.

Mike stood and crossed the room in two long strides. His hand gripped Ezekiel's like it was saving him from slipping off the earth. "Ezekiel, thank you for coming. I hope you can help us with the dilemma we're having."

Ezekiel wrenched his hand free and pulled off his coat; it was warm in the small room. "I hope that I can." He put his eyes on Robert. "What seems to be the problem, Bobby?"

It was not his imagination. A small smile formed on Robert's lips, a smile that illustrated his enjoyment more than anything. That smile caught Ezekiel off guard considering the state of his parents. "Why don't you tell him, Dad?"

Mike's face went as red as a summer-ripened tomato. He sucked in a breath through his nostrils and said in a near whisper, "He was drunk when he wrecked."

It was like a bucket of cold water had been thrown into Ezekiel's face. *Drunk?* What the hell could the boy have been thinking? "Is that true, Bobby?" The emotion came clearly through Ezekiel's voice, but Robert failed to notice it.

"It is, indeed."

Ezekiel didn't know who was talking to him. The boy on the bed looked like Robert Arrington, but this was not the kid he'd been visiting with each Sunday for the last several weeks. This kid was a cocky smartass. "You feeling okay, Bobby?"

"I'm feeling liberated."

This brought a sob out of Lucy, a sound Ezekiel had never heard her make before. Ezekiel stared at Bobby, somehow able to ignore Lucy's pain, before turning to Mike. "I think I need to speak with him alone. Would that be all right?"

"Sure, it would. Come on, Mother."

Without the parents, Ezekiel could speak more candidly with his young friend. He walked right up to the bed and grabbed Bobby's ear and twisted it while yanking it down. Bobby cried out in pain, of course he did, and the smile was finally off his young face. "What the hell are you thinking, you little brat? Driving drunk? You're supposed to be getting advice from me and you never drank before those little afternoon sessions with me. Do you think your father is so stupid he won't begin to suspect?"

"He won't," Robert cried.

Ezekiel twisted his ear harder. Up to this point, the preacher had maintained the façade in front of Robert, but this show of ignorance had brought the darker side up to the surface. Robert was getting to see something that Ezekiel usually reserved for those closest to him or those he was about to kill. He wasn't sure yet if Robert was a part of the latter.

"I understand your father better than anyone. He will suspect. He will come and speak with me about this, ask me if I knew, and I will tell him I did. I will put every inch of blame on you that I can. You've already proven yourself untrustworthy and a rebellious annoyance, this will only strengthen that. And whatever you hope to gain by pretending that that man doesn't scare you, you will lose tenfold. He will take it out of your skin."

He pulled the boy's ear right up to his own mouth so

that his lips grazed it with each word. “If you don’t start acting like the good Christian boy you’re supposed to be, I will come back here and rip this fucking ear from your head with my own hands. Do you understand me?”

“Yes.” The word was barely audible over the beeps in the room and pounding of blood in Ezekiel’s own ears. He released the boy and stepped back, attempting to recover his breath.

Robert lay back, his hand, the uninjured one, clutching at his ear, his eyes wider than possible, stared at Ezekiel.

“Oh come on, it didn’t hurt that bad.” Ezekiel stepped out of the room and found Mike and Lucy waiting for him. Lucy’s eyes were huge and full to the brim with water. She stood a step back from Mike, the anger radiating out of him like heat from a furnace. Ezekiel didn’t quite make eye contact with her, but he did his best to assure her with a gesture of his head.

“What did he have to say for himself?” Mike asked.

“I had a good talk with your son, Mr. Arrington. I believe he has seen the error of his ways.”

“Drunk? You believe that? Did you know, Brother Ezekiel? Did you know he’d been drinking?” He let the last word out in a whisper as if someone else may hear it and think less of Mr. Arrington.

Ezekiel wasn’t surprised by the question, but he’d hoped to have more time to prepare for it than this. “What we talk about on Sunday afternoons is really between us, Mike. If I had known he was in any way risking his safety, I would have told you about it. You know I would have.”

That appeased Mike, at least for now. “Thank you, Ezekiel. I don’t know what has gotten into that boy, but when he gets home, I'm going to find out if I can beat it out."

"As well you should." Ezekiel placed a hand on the man's shoulder. "Let's pray." The three stood in the hallway of the hospital outside of Robert's room and bowed their heads. Ezekiel's hand groped out during the prayer and sought Lucy's. He squeezed it and felt a clutching tremble in her own.

Mike went back in the room, not waiting for his wife to follow. She watched him go and as soon as the door closed, clutched Ezekiel's hand with a ferocious fierceness. "I was so worried about you," she whispered, the sound mimicking the hissing of the machines around the hospital. "I heard about the raid, and I was afraid you'd been caught."

"Oh no, sweetie, I'm just fine." The memory of the raid still haunted him, shaking him down to his core. It had been close, too close, and now he kept questioning everything. "But I've been thinking about you." He stepped closer and whispered in her ear words he hadn't said in years. "I think I love you."

She gasped and stepped back to search his eyes. She pulled her hand away, though not forcefully. "Ezekiel, this accident tonight has made me think a little about this. You have a more reckless side to you, and I'm beginning to wonder if that's worse for Robert than Mike. Right now, he may be the lesser of two evils."

The words struck a blow in the preacher's heart that resonated through the scars of his last lost love. "What are you saying?" he asked, though he knew.

"I don't think I can be with you anymore."

He started to reach for her hand, to pull her back to him, when Mike once more opened Robert's door and stuck his head out. "There you are. Still here, Brother?"

"I'm just leaving." The words, thick with emotion, nearly didn't make it out of his throat.

As he walked away from the hospital, his legs struggling with the process of taking him away from Lucy, he thought of the words he'd said, of the love he'd laid out for her. Her words, "the lesser of two evils," resonated with him and he wondered for the first time ever if he really was evil.

****

Lucy came by to see, not Mary, but Ezekiel. She cried in his living room, and Ezekiel didn't quite know how to respond. He'd been feeling quite a lot of emotion lately himself, but dealing with someone else's was maybe more than he could bear.

"Lucy?" He tentatively put a hand on her shoulder. "Are you all right?"

Her crying turned to sobs, but she did not shy from his touch. Instead she leaned right into him. Mary was off running her business, something that had caused a lot of contention in their marriage lately. So Lucy and Ezekiel had the entire house to themselves. He worked very hard to convince her to calm down.

"Lucy, you have to take a breath, and tell me what's going on."

Somehow she managed to get her sobs under control. Ezekiel extricated himself from her grip and got her something to drink. Between gulps of ice water, she managed to explain to her preacher why she had come over.

"It's Mike. I think I hate him."

Ezekiel sat on the couch next to her, listening to her story about her husband, the way he could suddenly turn abusive, how he was always so controlling, and now she feared for their young son. "How can I raise him in a house like that?" she asked. Her tears managed a reappearance when she spoke of her son.

While she spoke, Ezekiel thought of his own marriage, of the way that Mary's greed had soured their love. And the thing was, Ezekiel knew why she wanted to keep making and selling booze. He saw the freedom she enjoyed, but she wouldn't listen to his warnings, and it seemed she'd completely forgotten the reason they'd begun doing this in the first place.

Without realizing he'd spoken, he began to unload all of his own marital problems on Lucy. For her part, she listened, probably better than he had, and they each found that they finally had someone who understood.

They sat on the couch in the parsonage living room for two hours, talking, listening, laughing, and having one of the best days either one had had in a while. Lucy got up to leave. "I need to get back home. Mike will wonder where I've been."

Ezekiel stood with her. He offered her a hug and she gratefully leaned into his chest while he wrapped his arms around her. Her body felt small and fragile in his grip and he wanted to keep her there, to keep her safe. He loosened his grip and she looked up into his face. He locked eyes with her, and without thought, because thought would have stopped them, they brought their lips together over the expanse of all their pain and unhappiness. It was the first kiss.

When Ezekiel pulled away, he said,. "We probably shouldn't have done that."

"I, uh, don't know what happened." Lucy could not meet his eyes, but her fingertips trailed along her lips.

"I know what happened. We left ourselves in a vulnerable state, and our emotions took over. We'll have to be vigilant to not let it happen again. Now that a kiss has been shared, we'll be more inclined to share another."

"Oh, Ezekiel, you have such a way with words."

This time, there was no hesitation. Lucy took the lead, grabbing Ezekiel and planting her lips on his. Their second kiss felt more like the rest that would come to follow, like the awkwardness had slipped away, and all that was left was passion and lust.

Within a week, Ezekiel and Lucy had managed to share a bed together, and neither seemed to regret their risky act, and neither told their spouses.

Chapter 37

Ezekiel

The afternoon whirled away in a haze of moonshine and lamentations. Ezekiel did his best to dull the ache with booze, but it wasn't enough. He knew there was nothing that would help, that this pain would carry on with him for the rest of his life.

On his lap he held two pictures. On the right, a picture of Lucy Arrington, the woman who'd just pushed him out of her life. On the left, Mary Wilson, his first love, his wife, and the only woman he'd once believed he would ever love. The two women represented the happiest memories of his life, and the two most painful ones.

As he gazed into their eyes, the black and white photos not really doing them justice, he could hear the second hand on his watch ticking at the slower rate only known to those in extreme pain or extreme boredom. In the back of his mind, a thought attempted to rise up through the mirk of the booze, one that required Ezekiel's attention. He wasn't ready for it, but it came nonetheless.

His bootlegging empire was falling into dust around him. He was certain that Nigel Baxter would win and that he himself would be outed as the enemy of the people. The Baptist church would surely fall after that and a small Oklahoma town without a Baptist church might as well not be a town at all.

Without the House and without his constant flow of hooch, Ezekiel could guess that his career as a bootlegger was most certainly over, but the thought of returning to the pulpit, of being a preacher full-time, terrified him even more. He wasn't sure he could face God, the one he didn't believe in, if he had to return to that.

He pondered God as he drank, the burn helping him to accept the sins of his life. He'd spent his entire life believing in God, serving God, and pushing others into His embrace. However, one thing changed all that, forced his anger and pain into the forefront of his life, and took away his love for God.

Tears filled his eyes as he stared down at the photo of Mary. "I miss you. I miss life with you." The first teardrop splattered across her face with a resounding *plink.* He brought his gaze to Lucy. "I've lost everything I've loved. I want to get you back, but I don't know if I can."

Maybe he should seek the solace of a friend. He didn't have any, but he did have Johnny. He stood and swayed. Something tugged at him, urged him to the thick book lying nearly forgotten on a nearby table, but he ignored it. He didn't need that right now.

Chapter 38

Ezekiel

He didn't realize how much he loved her until he didn't have her. He'd trusted his heart to a married woman, and now he was paying the price. It made sense, he supposed, but there was something ever more depressing about the fact that he couldn't really talk to anyone about it.

Ezekiel did the two things he was best at when facing a difficult moment: he drank and he ran from the problem. This time, he ran to Wild Johnny's house. He, at least, wouldn't judge him for the affair; he would only judge him for falling in love.

Johnny's house was on the south end of town. It was a nice addition where most of the houses were still vacant. Johnny often talked of how he wished they'd stay that way, but of course, they wouldn't. The world continued to press on, changing with the times. Things they thought they would never see were now tolerated on a daily basis. It wouldn't be long before alcohol was legal in the state again, and probably not long after that anyone could buy whatever kind they wanted at the local grocery store.

Ezekiel tapped at the door, not sure what to expect. His head swam with the buzz of the hooch he'd been drinking in an attempt to dull the ache. But when Johnny opened the door, a smile stretching across his face when he saw Ezekiel, he knew he'd made the right choice.

Johnny stepped back, presenting the living room to the preacher. "Boss, what brings you out here?" he said as the door swung open.

Ezekiel rubbed his hands together in the warmth of Johnny's house. March in Oklahoma meant that you could never tell what the temperature would be or how much wind you should plan on dealing with. Today happened to be fairly cool coupled with a strong wind that brought the chill of the North with it. Frankly, it was miserable to be outside today.

This was Ezekiel's first time being inside Johnny's house. He tried to stay away from here in case someone might see him. But right now, none of that mattered.

"Johnny, I needed a friendly face. Hope I didn't interrupt you from doing anything."

Johnny smiled again, seeming genuinely happy to see the preacher. "I have a gift for you," he said.

"Oh? And what would that be?"

"A business venture that may prove to be lucrative."

Ezekiel smiled this time. Just what he'd been thinking while knocking at Johnny's door. "Sure, Johnny, what is this time? Drugs? Gambling? How about marriage licenses to queers?"

"Nothing that ridiculous. How about prostitution?"

Ezekiel let out a bark of laughter that was louder than he intended. "Prostitution? You have to have girls for that. Girls willing to spread their legs for some gross clientele who can't get women without money. Then you have to talk those girls into giving you some of that money, because why? What reason could we possibly have that would convince a woman to give up some money that she worked for?"

"Well, boss, we arrange the dates, put the idea out there. We pay off the cops. We keep a permanent threat over the men. They see that if anything happens to our girls, it'll be worse for them. All that should be reason enough to give us some of the money."

"Yeah, and what about the girls?"

Johnny smiled. "Follow me."

Chapter 39

Ezekiel

Whatever Ezekiel expected to find in Johnny's spare room, it was not a young woman. She lay on the bed, staring blankly at the ceiling, or past the ceiling at something Ezekiel could not perceive. Ezekiel stopped in the doorway and stared at the scene before him.

"What have you done?" he asked Johnny in a voice barely above a whisper.

Johnny walked into the room ahead of Ezekiel and turned back with the biggest smile Ezekiel had ever seen on the man's face. "This is the way, boss. We've got to make money somehow, and I've never made money legally, so I figure, why not prostitution? I can find more women, and we can have them set up in different towns all over northwest Oklahoma. This could even be how I make my mark."

He said all of this with such excitement and passion, that had he been talking about anything else, anything at all, Ezekiel probably would have supported him, but he could not stop looking at the woman lying on the bed. She didn't seem to know where she was, or why she was there. Ezekiel could not imagine what Johnny could be thinking.

"Who is she?" Ezekiel finally managed to ask.

Johnny turned his attention to the woman on the bed.

"She's a drifter. New to town, came from California, I think. Dabbled in prostitution out there. I met her through Debbie over at the shoe store. Debbie knew I'd been looking for some new prospects, and thought this gal here would be perfect." He patted her leg and laughed.

"What's her name?"

Johnny stopped smiling. "Uh, Susan." Ezekiel could see that naming her made him more uncomfortable.

"Is she here of her own free will?"

"What do you mean? She's not tied up, is she? Soon, she'll understand the reason we need each other. Really, look at her, she's beautiful. She's going to make us a lot of money."

Ezekiel watched her as she lay prone on the bed. Suddenly, she seemed to realize she wasn't alone in the room and she turned her head toward them. The smile that had been playing at her lips left abruptly when she saw Johnny standing in the doorway. Then she locked eyes with Ezekiel.

"Well, she's seen you now, boss," Johnny said with a chuckle.

Ezekiel grabbed him and pulled him from the room. "What are you thinking, Johnny? This is the most reckless thing you've ever done. You can't let her know who I am."

"Relax, Ezekiel, she's too popped up to ever be able to recognize you."

Ezekiel did notice the sudden drop of the term boss from Johnny, but chose to let it slide. "Here's what I would do: pay her a ton of money and send her away."

Johnny wasn't smiling now. "I will not. This is my chance, and you're not taking that from me."

Despite all of his convictions suddenly kicking into gear, Ezekiel decided that this was not the time for this fight. He would simply encourage his young associate to release the woman. And he would hope that she wouldn't recognize him if she saw him out in town.

"Fine, but you must understand the extreme danger you put us in by bringing a person into this. She's clearly held as a prisoner and I could tell that she was afraid of you. If she escapes…"

"She won't!"

"I am simply saying, if she were to, you must see that she could go straight to the cops and you'd be done."

Johnny stood quiet as if contemplating the ideas behind this. "I'll be careful, boss, I promise. I'll make you proud."

As Ezekiel left, he wondered how in the world anyone could be proud of someone for forcing another person into prostitution. He would take care of this, he had to. But for the moment, he had a lot more to worry about.

Chapter 40

Nigel

On the following Tuesday morning, with little else to occupy his time, Nigel Baxter sat in the waiting room at the offices of the First Baptist Church. He wasn't sure what he expected to find here, but he hoped that another meeting with the preacher might yield some results. His name kept coming up in conversations.

However, it seemed the preacher was not around. Wanda, the nice older lady who pretended to do secretarial jobs while reading newspapers, let him sit in comfortable silence while he waited on the preacher's return.

"Did he say how long he would be out?" Nigel asked.

"He had some people to visit this morning. Mike Arrington's boy just got out of the hospital yesterday, so he may be out visiting their house. Hard to tell."

Nigel nodded. Mike Arrington seemed to be the preacher's closest friend. Or at least a strong leader in the church. He pulled out his notepad and made a note to meet with Mr. Arrington. That man could also have some answers.

The door opened and a cold wind blew the preacher through the door. "Hello, Wanda. Glad to be inside today? It is mighty cold out there." He pulled his hat and coat off to hang on the coat rack beside the door.

"I sure am, though if that door keeps opening up, it won't be that different."

Ezekiel chuckled then turned to find Nigel waiting for him. He didn't seem at all surprised to see him. "Hello there, Mr. Baxter, I didn't see you. Are you waiting for me?"

Nigel stood. "Yes, sir, if it's no trouble."

"No trouble at all. Give me a moment to get settled."

"If it's all the same, this won't take a minute of your time."

The preacher stared into Nigel's eyes. "All right then. Follow me."

The two sat in Ezekiel's office, each on his own side of the desk. "So what brings you around, Nigel?"

Nigel noticed the loss of the formal tone from the preacher. He let it roll off. "I just keep hearing your name pop up around the town and thought I might need to stop back by and speak with you. Maybe get to know you a little more."

"Sure, sure. Who's been talking about me this time? That police chief? The mayor?"

"Well, yes, but most recently from a woman named Lucy."

"Oh yes? And what would Lucy be asking about me?"

"She seems to be in love with you. Is the feeling mutual?"

Ezekiel let out a chuckle. "Mr. Baxter, Lucy is a married woman, and I'm sure you noticed the ring on her finger as evidence. I would not so readily break one of the Ten Commandments."

Nigel pulled his well-beaten notepad from his inner

pocket and flipped a couple of pages. “Married, you say? I saw no ring on the day she spoke to me. I wonder if she would have some reason for concealing that.”

Ezekiel shook his head. “Like all married women, I’m certain there are times she takes the ring from her finger and forgets to return it. It doesn’t mean anything malicious.”

After jotting down a couple of notes, Nigel nodded. “She also seemed concerned that I may have arrested you in the raid on the speakeasy. Do you have any idea why that would be?”

Ezekiel’s eyes stayed steady. Nothing could surprise this man today. “I went there from time to time to see which of my patrons might be there. You have to understand that I only went for my flock. A shepherd must occasionally leave the field to find the missing members of the flock, so I, too, must do so.”

“That is a lovely sentiment, sir, but don’t you worry about your public image, being seen out there? Why not report the place to the police if you knew about it?”

The preacher considered the questions, drumming his index finger on the top of his desk. “Why, the police already knew about it. I saw some of the officers out there myself. And if an officer of the law can enter such an establishment and not worry about his reputation, surely a preacher can, too.” He waved a hand in the direction of Nigel. “But we don’t need to worry about any of that now, do we?”

Nigel nodded again, smiling slightly. Calling out the police in this matter was quite an interesting move. He couldn’t place what was odd about Mr. Ezekiel Wilson. He’d never met a Baptist preacher with as strong of a stance against alcohol, but didn’t report the presence of a speakeasy in town, even though he knew exactly where to go and how to get in. Maybe it was nothing. Maybe the preacher really did like to go out there and pray for his people, encouraging them to leave the bottle. Or maybe he enjoyed the bottle himself.

Maybe he liked men the way Edward Young did and he went to see that little man.

That was a nasty thought and Nigel shoved it from his mind forcefully.

"Do you partake in alcohol, Mr. Wilson?"

Ezekiel leaned back and a fire came into his eyes. "I think you asked me that at the diner on the day we met. Now if this is simply going to be a review of what we already know, you might as well get out of here. I've got work that I need to do."

Nigel held up a hand. "Mr. Wilson, I understand your frustration, I simply wanted to find out if the answer was the same today as it was that day."

"Of course it's the same. I don't drink and I never have."

Nigel had him angry and now wanted to catch him off guard. "You have an altar call each week at the end of your service, don't you?"

"What? I, er, yes we do. It's a chance for sinners to come clean in the House of God with an ordained minister there to pray for them."

"And what happens if no one comes forward?"

"What do you mean?"

"I mean, do you stand there awkwardly, waiting for people who either don't need your prayer or don't want it?"

Ezekiel stood and slammed a fist into the middle of the desk. A resounding boom echoed around the room.

"Mr. Baxter." The words should have come out as a yell, but they were quiet, much quieter after the boom of the desk. "If you want to come in here and ask me questions, you better refrain from insulting me while you do it. I have never coerced anyone into coming forward during the alter call. If they do, it is because the Lord has so moved them."

"Now Mr. Wilson, I never said that." Nigel's smile didn't leave his face. "You simply jumped to that conclusion."

"You think I don't know what people say about me? I've been here far too long to not hear it all. I do not need some out-of-towner to come into my town and tell me what I already know." His face was red and flecks of spit dotted the top of his desk from the force of his words.

Nigel did not seem to mind as he listened to Ezekiel's tirade. In fact, he found it rather enlightening. "Mr. Wilson, I believe I'm seeing a different side of you that most people don't get to see."

Ezekiel's face flushed and all the fight went out of him. He sat back in his chair, deflating like a blown tire. "You've managed to find the one thing that gets under my skin." He sighed, a deep rolling breath that cooled his temper like a strong north wind. "I do apologize for my outburst. I am a passionate man, and sometimes, that passion spills over."

"I can see that, but it is probably I who should apologize. I have no reason to be asking so much of you. You're not a suspect or anything. Really, I'll just go and get out of your way."

Ezekiel stared at him, letting a silence fall between them. At last he said, "Thank you for stopping by, Inspector. I hope your search proves fruitful."

Nigel walked out of the office and out of the church unsure of how to feel about the meeting. If he'd been talking with a suspect in an interrogation room, he would have expected the type of behavior he'd just seen. He had a tough time believing he'd just met with a pastor.

Maybe he should keep a closer eye on Ezekiel Wilson. Nigel lit a cigarette before getting back into his car, the smoke burning a little heat back into his limbs.

Chapter 41

Robert

Things couldn't possibly get any worse. Robert had managed to piss off everyone he knew, including the one man he thought would be most impressed with him, Ezekiel Wilson. Resting in his own bed, his arm propped on an extra pillow, he allowed himself the time to think on the mistakes of the past few days. He stared at the ceiling and thought about the possibility of going to jail. When the officer had come to the hospital to visit them and break this bad news to him, he'd finally begun to grasp the full implications of his actions. Robert replayed the scene in his mind.

The officer removed his hat when he entered the hospital room. He said, "We just wanted you all to be aware of the possibility of jail time. Could be ninety days to two years, I think." That let the air out of the room and all the confidence that Robert had been feeling since waking up in the hospital went with it. "I think I can help you out, though."

This perked Mike up and stopped Lucy's sobs. The officer continued, "Tell us where you got the hooch."

Robert stared defiantly back at the officer, shocked at the sudden demand. "And if I refuse?"

The officer sighed. "I've already told you, you'll likely go to jail. Alcohol is illegal in Oklahoma, remember? You should probably consider that kind of thing before you make stupid decisions." He turned to Robert's parents. "He will be arrested as soon as he's released from the hospital. Unless he gives us a name. See if you can get something out of him."

An ultimatum. Robert didn't actually believe they would put him in jail. He wasn't eighteen, after all, but he wasn't sure what they would do to him. He glanced over at his dad and wondered if jail wouldn't be better than whatever the old man had in store for him. He'd never seen such anger and disappointment on the faces of his parents.

Mike pulled a chair over beside the bed so that he could look Robert in the eye. He sighed. "I won't tell you what you have to do, but I'll tell you what you *should* do. I don't care where you got it, but you need to think about your life. If you ever wanted to go to college or do anything outside of working for me, you better consider giving up whoever it is. Your life will be gone if you have a conviction on your record. No one will hire you."

It was the most level-headed thing he'd heard out of his dad's mouth since the accident, maybe ever. His dad was actually appealing to his desire to leave the farm. It was an inconceivable idea. Robert felt lost without the invincible feeling he'd been riding since the wreck, and with his own dad treating him more like a son and less like shit, Robert knew what he had to do.

Now in his bedroom at home, he knew his decision would carry great weight with it. Someone would go to jail, but it wouldn't be him. Then again, it was still possible that jail would be better.

A knock at the door interrupted his thoughts. Without awaiting a response, Mike entered and stared down at his son. "Come into the living room. You have some visitors."

As Robert left the safety of his bedroom, pain shooting through his arm as he took each step, he didn't know what he expected to see. But when he saw Becky sitting with her parents on his couch, he found he could no longer walk or speak. One thought ran through his head: "What new horror is this?"

Becky's parents sipped from coffee mugs, steam rising up around their faces. Her mother stared down at the floor, but when Robert entered the room, her father's eyes locked on him. Mr. Lewis had always been kind to Robert, allowing him to take his daughter all around town without much of a curfew. Now, however, Mr. Lewis' eyes were shot through with bright red veins and the edges were swollen and purple. The hand that clutched the coffee mug turned white and shook slightly.

Becky held no coffee mug, but she also stared down at the floor like her mother. Tears slid steadily down her cheeks. Robert kept his eyes on her, his heart jumping up and down his chest like some over-excited jackrabbit. He willed her to silently give him some clue as to the reason for this meeting.

"Here he is," Mike said when he entered the room behind Robert.

Mrs. Lewis brought her gaze to him. She looked hollow, like someone who'd spent the day learning they would not live much longer. "Robert, you may want to sit down." Her voice did not carry any of the sweet tones it normally did for him. She was a dear lady who always seemed happy to see Robert and, unlike Robert's own parents, enjoyed the fact that Robert and Becky were dating.

"I'm afraid you may not be so pleased to see us," Mrs. Lewis said to Robert once he'd taken his seat. Mr. Lewis remained silent, only watching through those purple-rimmed eyes. "Becky," Mrs. Lewis continued, "would you like to tell them?"

Becky shook her head. Robert wanted to go to her and hold her, take away whatever pain had caused those tears. This was his Becky.

Mrs. Lewis watched her daughter. "Now, Becky, tell him."

Again Becky shook her head, unleashing a new torrent of tears. Mrs. Lewis turned her daughter toward her and slapped her, open-handed across the face. For the first time since Robert had entered the room, Becky met someone's eyes, her mother's. She held her mother's gaze, the tears drying with the sting of the slap. She held a hand to her reddening cheek, anger springing up through her mask of sorrow she'd been wearing. Robert had never seen anything like it cross his girl's face.

Then Becky turned, still holding her face, to look into Robert's eyes. He saw there within them the love she felt for him and the pain, the hurt that now coursed through the room. She didn't move, didn't speak, but gathered her courage to the news she must deliver. He was close enough to touch her, but had never felt farther from her.

"What is it, Becky?" he asked, a tremble coming into his voice.

Then she let loose two words that would forever change everything. "I'm pregnant."

Chapter 42

Ezekiel

In the dark of the secret basement room, supplies were running low. Ezekiel rubbed a cold glass of moonshine across his forehead before he took another swig. During the process of taking inventory, he'd nearly burned the house and church down three times. He kept seeing the face of Nigel Baxter in front of him. "That lousy bastard coming into *my* church and questioning *my* methods?" He kept thinking it on a loop as he stared into the abyss.

Still he did have to hand it to the guy. He'd already learned so much in the few weeks of being in town, had happened across Edward Young and convinced him to spill…what? How much had the little man told the inspector?

It hadn't even occurred to Ezekiel until this moment, but now that the thought had entered his mind, he wondered where it had been. What had Edward told the police? Was it simply about the House or was there more? Had Ezekiel Wilson been named? If so, why hadn't he been arrested?

He slammed the rest of the moonshine down his throat, the liquid burning like fire all the way down to his gut. He did not cough or sputter; he was a man who'd grown used to the burn.

He stared into the glass, watched the ice cubes tumble over each other as they melted like the last of his empire. His soul smelled of rot. He'd left that poor girl to be a prisoner to a man with the moniker of Wild. For the first time in many years, Ezekiel felt guilt.

Guilt had once been a good friend. It wasn't easy to grow up as a Baptist, knowing that whatever you did would never be good enough to the adults who'd all done it before you. The young Ezekiel strived for perfection because the leaders of his church made him believe it was not only attainable, but expected. Of course, now he knew better, and the knowing killed the guilt, that and a denial of a higher authority.

The booze made his head swim.

He sat on a crate of beer. It was the last crate of beer, and he thought he could maybe sell it for three times its value, but who would sell it? Several of his runners had already been arrested. Since the night at the House, two more of his crew had gone down. Along with them, he'd lost several hundred dollars in booze, booze that the cops were probably drinking right now.

He heard Johnny coming down the stairs before he saw the man, and knew it was him because of the boots he wore. Johnny'd grown up in southern Kansas working on cattle ranches. He still did from time to time just to remember what it felt like. He kept the boots as a reminder of his past, a sentiment that Ezekiel had always admired.

"Afternoon, Johnny."

"How'd you know it was me, boss?"

"Them shit-kickers you've got on, same as always."

Johnny smiled at the affectionate name for his cowboy boots. The smile didn't quite light up his face as it normally would have.

"What's wrong?" Ezekiel asked.

"Boss, I think something bad's happening. Four or five cop cars just went out to the Arrington farm. Charles King is working out there today. I think they're going for him."

The glass slipped free from Ezekiel's grip and hit the concrete below without him noticing. Not Charles. Aside from Johnny, Charles was one of the few who knew Ezekiel was behind it all. "Why didn't you find out sooner?"

He shifted his feet, unable to meet the preacher's eyes. "We've no police left on the force who take money from us. We can't tell who's coming and who's going."

"So why would they be going for Charles?"

Johnny took a deep breath. "Best I got, someone snitched on him." He shrugged and took a look around at the limited amount of inventory.

Ezekiel rubbed his chin, his eyes focusing on the fallen glass, the ice melting into a small puddle on the ground. In his years of building up his booze empire, slowly taking out the competition, he'd never had a single person, no matter how degraded or disturbed, snitch on one of his men. It was an unheard of practice. It would be like fucking in church: you just didn't do it. "Who would have the nerve? Who in the world could do such a thing?"

Johnny shook his head. "I don't know. My speculation only goes so far."

Ezekiel wanted to scream. What was the point in having Johnny around if he was going to let things like this happen? Somehow, he maintained his composure and didn't cram his fist down Johnny's throat. Instead he flared his nostrils and blew the anger out with a lungful of air. He kept his eyes locked on his right-hand man.

"We have to get him. We killed Edward, we'll kill Charles. Then, well, I don't know what then, but at the very least, I'll stay out of prison. You have to get me into him."

"You know it won't be that easy, boss. It can't be, not after Edward."

Ezekiel stood and kicked the glass into the wall. What was left disintegrated, throwing shards of glass and flecks of booze all over the two men. "Is there nothing we can do?"

Johnny shifted his feet, cleared his throat, and dropped his eyes. "Charles won't talk. We've groomed him for this. What we need to do more than worry about him is find out who ratted on him and get that guy. That'll send a message."

He nodded at Johnny. "Yeah, see that it gets done. I don't want you on the streets tonight, though. Go home. Send one of your lackeys to do it. You still have that girl?"

Johnny smiled. "Susan? Yeah, boss. You want to come see her again?"

"Cut the crap." The smile dropped from Johnny's face. "I want you to give her money and send her on. Tell her she has to leave town. And if we find out she went to the cops, we'll kill her."

"Boss, you can't be serious."

"You've never questioned me before." Ezekiel took a step forward and put a hand on Johnny's shoulder. "All this time, all the bodies we've buried, and now you question me about this?"

"This could be a good opportunity for us."

Ezekiel slapped Johnny across the face then put his hand back on his shoulder. “Do what I say. I don’t give direct orders so you can ignore them.”

Johnny stood in silence, clearly not wanting to rub the sting out of his cheek. At last he nodded and turned to leave.

Ezekiel listened as the boots clumped back up the stairs. Once the younger man was gone, he went upstairs himself for a drink of cold water. He missed Lucy terribly at that moment and decided he should call her. But when he reached for the phone, it rang.

“Hello?” Ezekiel said into the receiver.

“Brother Ezekiel.” The voice coming through the phone made the preacher quiver, he had never heard such anger rippling through it before. For a moment, he thought that maybe Lucy had told her husband. “This is Mike Arrington. We’re home from the hospital.” He cleared his throat. “I haven’t called you since we got home, because, well, I found out,” he paused and cleared his throat, “I found out I’m going to be a grandfather.” He didn’t say this with the warmth and cheer that most people would, instead he said it with sadness and a barely controlled rage under the surface. “I thought you should know.” His voice broke on the last word and Ezekiel could hear the man fighting off sobs. “I really hoped you would be able to help him, but he just keeps getting worse. He started by lying to me. Now he’s drinking and having premarital sex. I don’t know if I can beat it out of him, but I’m going to try.”

Ezekiel rubbed at his temple, a slight tremor in his hand. “Mike, I know you’re in pain right now, but that’s not the best course of action is it?” Ezekiel’s mind reeled, searching for the right words to say here. This was his fault, spurring the boy on for his own entertainment.

Mike sighed. "Maybe not. But I can tell you that we'll be in church on Sunday morning, and you can bet that boy will be up front to pray with you."

"An excellent idea, Mike. I'll come out to visit you guys soon. Maybe I can visit with Robert for a while."

"That would be great. The police just left. They took Charles King."

The preacher took a breath and sputtered, "Charles arrested?"

"Yes. Maybe the only good thing to come from this. It seems he was the one providing booze to my boy. Robert admitted to it to help ease the Hell he's put us through. I never want to see that Australian bastard again."

It was unusual to hear Mike curse, but Ezekiel didn't even notice. His mind was bent around the fact that it was Robert; the boy who'd been coming to his house every week had betrayed Charles King to the cops. Somehow Ezekiel got off the phone, promising to come out to the Arrington farm soon. He pictured plunging a knife into the boy's throat. It seemed heartless, but it might be the only way to approach the situation.

Chapter 43

Nigel

Charles King sat in the chief's office where Nigel had recently broken a cop's finger. He was shackled to the chair he sat in, but Nigel felt no threat in speaking to this young man. He stared straight ahead, chewing a piece of gum with the intensity of a cow chewing its cud.

"Mr. King, thank you for coming down here today."

The chewing continued. A blank stare just above Nigel's head.

"So I see that you're Australian. What brought you here to America?"

Still chewing. Still staring. Nigel was not bothered by this, in fact he expected it.

"I've never been to Australia myself. Hear it's nice. Not sure why anyone would want to leave there. Especially for a small town in Oklahoma. Me? I'd rather be anywhere than this godforsaken state. Probably find better women and better booze in other places. Like California. I think their laws are pretty lenient. But stay out of Utah."

He smiled at Charles, who continued to stare at the spot above his head. Nigel had hoped that by talking poorly about the state, he would pull some words out of Charles. It hadn't worked, so he decided to get down to business.

"OK, Mr. King, I can see that you're not going to be giving up any information freely. So I'm going to tell you what's happening. Man by the name of Edward Young gave me your name."

Charles' eyes moved, dropped from that spot above Nigel's head to stare into the inspector's own eyes. He sought the truth in the statement, wondering if he dare believe it. Nigel attempted to show him the seriousness of the situation.

"The late Edward Young promised more names, but was unfortunately killed before he could give them to me. You don't know anything about that, do you?"

Charles' eyes grew wide. "I didn't kill nobody." Those were the first words he spoke in front of Nigel and the inspector was impressed by the loss of his accent.

"Now, Charles, I'm not saying you did. I'm asking *if* you did. Did you kill Mr. Young?"

"No." The chains around his arms rattled with nervous energy.

"We are getting somewhere, aren't we?"

Charles stared at the table now, the chewing of the gum ceased for the moment.

"Have you ever distributed illegal substances in the state of Oklahoma?"

"Shouldn't be illegal," he mumbled to the table.

"I'm sorry, Mr. King, but I didn't quite catch that."

He sat up straighter and met Nigel's eyes once more. "I said it shouldn't be illegal."

"Your opinion on the legality of the substance is not in question here. In the state of Oklahoma, it is illegal. So you're admitting to transporting alcohol?"

"I didn't say that." He brought his arms up onto the table and stared down at his hands. They were rough and dirty. Clearly the hands of a working man.

"Seems you implied it, whether stated directly or not."

"Am I really in trouble?"

The question was almost funny to Nigel. He suppressed the laugh that jumped up his throat. "Yes. You are. You could lose your green card and we could ship you back to Australia. You have some options to keep that from happening, so I would suggest that you participate."

Charles shook his head. "You can't send me back there." The accent, without his consent, came back to his voice and for the first time since he started speaking, Nigel could hear the "Down Under" in the tone.

"We can. We can do a lot more than you would suspect. You came into our country and broke our laws, no matter how stupid you think they are. We have every right to kick you out of here."

Charles took a deep breath, concentrated on once more hiding his accent. "What do I have to do?"

Nigel leaned forward. "Sign a confession. Then I want names. Those over you. Who are you working for?"

Charles thought about it. "You can have the confession." He nodded. "I sold plenty of illegal alcohol. Moonshine and liquor and beer. Some I bought in Kansas and transported down here. Some of it was locally made. You've been trying to shut them down, but they're still churning out booze. One guy is named Hank Thomas."

Nigel leaned farther into the table. "Hank Thomas is missing."

"Is he? Well, I haven't been to see him for a while. He must've bolted when he heard about you. He was like a cat, always jumpy when something new came around."

Nigel stared at the man, wondering what game he was playing. "You may have bought booze from Hank Thomas, but who hired you to buy it? Who do you work for?"

Charles smiled. "You're not paying attention, Mr. Inspector. My last name tells you who I work for: King. I am the King and I work for no man."

The smile that coupled with the statement made Nigel even angrier. He couldn't let this little Australian punk talk to him like this. He stood and leaned across the table to put his face directly in front of Charles'. The hold on his temper began to slip like it did with the police officer. He wanted to punch the smile directly off this man's face. But for the moment, he held.

"You do not understand the seriousness of the situation. You cannot. I know you're no crime lord. You work for someone. I will find out who, and when I do, you will be shipping off, setting sail for a new world."

The smile never wavered. He kept his eyes locked on Nigel's. "It's fine if you don't believe me. But I'm telling the truth."

Nigel nodded and walked out of the room. He had paperwork to fill out, a confession to type up, and a prisoner to transport to the county jail. He would harass this bastard until he spilled everything. He would also need to beef up security at the jail to ensure that he would still be alive in the morning.

Nigel ran a hand through his hair. He could feel he was getting closer to the end of this.

Chapter 44

Ezekiel

The desk in front of Ezekiel felt more expansive than ever. He stared at the stuff that littered it and wondered about the notes, the Bible, the pictures of lives gone past, the evidence that he'd once been a good man, a man of integrity. He had a list of people he needed to call or maybe even visit in person. But today, he wanted to soak up the atmosphere of his office, a place he'd always managed to find peace.

He heard the door to the church offices open. He heard Wanda wish someone a good morning. Footsteps neared his door and he waited patiently for whoever it was to knock. When it happened at last, he said, "Come in."

The door opened and Ezekiel's least favorite deacon stepped in. It was so much more difficult to see Mike now that Lucy had ended things with him. Seeing Mike and knowing she chose him instead of Ezekiel when their affair had been going strong for so long, made things hurt that much more.

"Brother Mike," Ezekiel started, but stopped when he realized the deacon was not alone. Behind him stood a young woman who seemed vaguely familiar. "What's this?"

Mike held the woman gently by the hand and guided

her into the room. She stared at the floor and moved so feebly, Ezekiel became concerned that if Mike let her go, she would simply fall to the floor. "Brother Ezekiel, this woman needs your help. She hasn't said much, just that she needs to go into hiding."

Ezekiel stood and walked toward the two in his office doorway. At long last, the woman, Susan was her name, looked up at Ezekiel and her eyes grew in sudden alarm. "No!" she shouted and attempted to pull away from Mike.

"Girl, what's gotten into you?" Mike asked as he struggled to keep a hold of her.

Ezekiel knew then where he'd seen her. Knew that Johnny had not let her go, but that she had escaped, the very thing he swore wouldn't happen. And now, Mike brought her here.

Mike kept his hands on her as she struggled violently to get away. Everything Ezekiel had been afraid of when he'd entered that room at Johnny's was happening now. Not only had she escaped, she recognized Ezekiel. Here, after years of work, keeping everything quiet about his secret life, all would be undone by this woman.

"Mike, what is going on with her?" Ezekiel asked.

"It's him," Susan roared. Tears streamed freely down her face.

"It's who, honey?" Mike asked gently, but still firmly holding onto her. Suddenly her eyes rolled up into the back of her head and her body went limp.

Ezekiel stepped forward and helped Mike bring her to the couch in his office. "What in the world was that about?" Mike asked. He stared down at the woman, rubbing his hands together as if trying to get them clean of her.

"I wish I knew, Mike. You said she needed help?"

"Yes, I believe she was being held against her will. I could've taken her to the police, but I thought it might be easier for her to come here. I guess I was wrong."

Ezekiel nodded. "You never know how people may react to church. I think you did the right thing, regardless, Mike. You said you brought her straight here?"

"Well, she was insistent that we stop at the post office and deliver a letter. I'm not sure who it was to, but she seemed to think it was of vital importance."

Ezekiel absorbed this information, then nodded. "Leave her here. She can rest on the couch, and I'll contact some of the women in the church to come and care for her. That should ease her. Would your wife be available?"

Mike continued to watch Susan. "Of course she would, Brother Ezekiel. Anything to help."

Ezekiel smiled and shook Mike's hand. "You're a good man, Mike. Don't worry about her, I'll take care of it."

Mike turned toward the office door and began to leave. He paused at the door and turned back for one last look at Susan. "That was a strange way for her to act, wasn't it?"

"Yes, it was."

"I wonder if I shouldn't take her somewhere else."

Ezekiel smiled, but without joy. If Mike had looked at the smile, he may have been reminded of a shark. "Mike, don't worry about her. I promise you, I'll take care of her. Who knows better than a pastor what a person needs?"

That seemed to calm Mike. "Of course. That's why

I brought her here in the first place. Thank you."

At last, Mike slipped out of the office door, and Ezekiel closed it behind him. He turned back to Susan inert on the couch. This seemed to be the greatest stroke of luck in Ezekiel's life. Mike could have taken her to the police in which case, it would be a short time before Johnny would be arrested for these crimes. Ezekiel knew he need not worry about Johnny spilling his guts, however, it would be the biggest blow to his business if Johnny got arrested.

He would not call Johnny to help with this. He would have to take care of Susan on his own. First thing was to get her out of his office.

He stepped into the hallway and saw that lunch had come, so Wanda would not be in the building. The music and youth ministers' office doors were closed. Another stroke of luck. He had to move her before it ran out.

He went to the backdoor of the church and peered out. No cars in the parking lot, no one in the alley. Just a short fifty yards to his house, and he would have her.

He went back to his office and lifted Susan's body from the couch. She barely broke a hundred pounds. He carried her out of his office and down the hallway. Susan moaned softly in that far off world of sleep. Ezekiel made it to the backdoor, took a deep breath, and made his way to his house.

Somehow, in some miraculous way, Ezekiel made it home without incident. He carried Susan into the basement and managed to get her locked into the spare room when she finally woke up. She screamed for a while, but Ezekiel knew that no one would hear her. He went back into the church with a smile on his face that something had finally run so smoothly.

When he entered his office, he found Lucy sitting there, waiting for him. His heart jumped into overtime at the sight of her. “Lucy?” he said.

She turned to him, and she smiled, but not her normal, full smile that filled every room with her light. It was a reluctant smile, as if she didn’t quite know what the situation might bring.

“Hi, Brother Ezekiel, Mike called me and said you might need some help here at the church. I drove the new work truck down here. He seemed to think it was a pretty big deal.”

“Ah, well, it wasn’t as important as he seemed to think it was.”

“Okay.” She stood and turned toward the office door. “Well, if you don’t need my help.”

She stepped toward him, and he reached out to her. “Lucy,” he said.

“No, Ezekiel, stop. We’re past that, I’ve told you.”

“Have you told Mike about our affair?”

She scoffed at him. “Do you think you’d still be standing if he knew about us?”

“Do you really think Mike would resort to violence?”

Lucy laughed, a sound completely without joy. “He already has. Did you never listen to Robert when he told you stories? But please, just let me go.”

Ezekiel watched her leave. His heart couldn’t quite take the sight of her walking away from him.

Chapter 45

Robert

As March began to dwindle away, Robert's arm felt better. He had the idea that it would be healed up enough to graduate without a cast. Not that he cared. Graduation was the furthest thing from his mind. His dad had been working him harder than ever and with one arm, it seemed to take twice as long. Then there was the fact that it was impossible to go back to life before the Fall Festival. He'd tasted sin and now he wanted more.

Because of what he'd done, however, his freedoms were greatly limited. He could no longer drive by himself. He worked most hours with his father by his side and could only drink water from a clear glass. He had to spend two hours each night at the dining room table, working on his schoolwork. His grades bounced back up rapidly, still he missed alcohol and the way it made him feel.

But what he missed most was Rebecca Lewis.

The announcement of her pregnancy had thrown his entire world off kilter. He couldn't quite cope with the amount of things that happened in such a quick progression. Her parents had brought her to his house to tell him because they wanted her to say goodbye to him, to know that it was his fault that she had to go away.

She moved off north to South Dakota with her aunt,

her dad's sister. The plan was to keep her there until the baby was born, then the child would be put up for adoption and Becky could return home, if she chose.

Of all the things he missed from the sins he'd committed, it wasn't the sin he missed, it was her. Her smile, her presence, her conversation. They'd shared an English class together that felt smaller and less enjoyable without her. *Everything* was less enjoyable without her.

The work at home was always blessedly difficult which allowed his mind to focus on the task. Still, he began to devise a plan for leaving, for escaping, for finding his girl and their child. His heart swelled when he thought of being a father. He became determined to be a better dad than his own had ever been to him.

When everything he'd done had finally come to light, Robert had felt compelled to rat out Charles King. He pretended to not be affected by the arrest of the man he'd considered a friend and confidant, but he was. He missed Charles almost as much as he missed Becky. He'd been able to be himself around the Australian and had enjoyed the feeling of not being judged for his desires and the sins that came from them. He greatly missed that, and probably, missed that the most.

With his dad always lurking, silently judging him, he could not freely be himself. That was the greatest restriction on his freedom: his dad.

Mike Arrington had become like his own shadow. The only time Mike wasn't at the farm, Robert was at school. And on occasion, Mike would swing by the school to check on his son, make sure he was attending the classes he needed to graduate high school. He became determined to have a successful son.

One-armed and working harder than he ever had in

his life, Robert again lost himself in his work until his father interrupted him.

"I keep thinking I need to hire another worker to replace Charles, but with the way you've been working, I think I just need to wait until you get that cast off. It'll be like having three workers hired here." He cut a chunk of apple with his pocket knife and slipped the piece between his teeth.

Robert didn't look up. In fact, he had little to say to his father since the car accident. Most of his speeches were confined to one or two words. This time however, he decided he could no longer take the man's pointless conversation.

"Charles is probably going to be thrown in jail and at least be deported for selling alcohol and you talk about it casually."

Mike's eyes grew wide at the statement, but crinkled again as he smiled. "I hope he does go to jail, giving my boy an illegal substance like that."

Robert thrust the pitchfork he'd been using aside. "And how do you think I feel, huh? That kind of thing hanging over my head. I'll always be responsible for that man going to jail. And I liked Charles. He'll never speak to me again and you're talking about what he deserves."

Mike held up a hand the hand clutching the knife as if to hold back the anger in his son. "You are not responsible for his actions, boy; he did this to himself. Just because you did the right thing and turned him in, that doesn't make you guilty of his jail time. Use your head, boy, or what's left of it."

"You know nothing!"

Those three words caused Mike's eyes to turn red and his whole face to shake with anger. He threw the apple at Robert which hit him square in the nose then came at him with his fist raised. He slipped the knife back into his pocket before he started in on his son; he wouldn't want to use the wrong hand. Three, four times, he slammed his fist into Robert's head. Robert fell to the ground, attempting to block the blows to his head with his arms. Mike began kicking him then, the point of his boot catching Robert in the ribs and the stomach, forcing bursts of air out of him.

While he kicked him, he shouted, "I. Know. Nothing? I. Know. Nothing?" Each word punctuated with a kick. It wasn't the first beating Robert had ever gotten from his father, but it was the worst.

Chapter 46

Ezekiel

A person walking amongst broken glass should tread carefully. Each step must be deliberate to escape the torn flesh that would result from a misplaced step. Ezekiel viewed that image as a proper metaphor for his life as of late. And at the moment, he could feel his feet bleeding from not being careful enough.

The arrest of Charles King had been a blow to him as it was the first arrest of someone who could name him as the kingpin. So far, Charles had remained quiet on the subject of who he worked for, however, and Nigel Baxter had started the paperwork to get him deported. Johnny had been able to coerce some information out of a new police officer who'd had a history he wouldn't want his new bosses finding out about. Ezekiel was sure the deportation paperwork was a ruse to get the man to confess. Ezekiel, who had had enough experience with the Inspector, didn't agree. Nigel intended to ship him off with or without a confession.

Johnny and Ezekiel had been working on a plan to bust Charles out, but their main focus was to murder Nigel. With the rise in arrests, the sale of booze had evaporated. Ezekiel's secret basement room was all but empty and his customer base had turned cold to the idea of buying. Of course Ezekiel had plenty of money, but that was not the point. He had to show his strength. If Nigel Baxter ended up dead, no one would question the authority of the unknown kingpin again.

He'd been expecting Johnny for an hour and his right-hand man still had yet to show. Nothing to worry about, Ezekiel assured himself. He had plenty of other things with which to concern himself.

His church had begun to notice his lack of concentration behind the podium on Sunday mornings. His preaching had shortened and become less impassioned. Of course there were those who favored a shortened sermon as it got them to lunch sooner, but the deacons had expressed their concern and even suggested he take a vacation, something he had never done during his time as the preacher in town.

But a vacation did sound nice. Something had changed in him since Susan had come into his office. He'd managed to get her into his basement without anyone noticing, and since then, he'd spoken to her. He'd confided in her. And it made him *feel* again. That was something he hadn't really managed to do since Mary died.

He'd been able to share with Susan the story of his affair with Lucy, his leap into crime, and his deep and abiding hatred of himself. He could reveal secrets and remove masks with her, something he hadn't done in at least a decade.

Now he descended the steps to his basement and found Susan asleep on the bed he'd moved there for her. She was a peaceful sleeper and indeed the two had helped each other over the last few days. He'd helped her explore the feelings of hatred and betrayal that she felt toward her family. And she'd helped him explore the untouched feelings he'd buried with Mary.

No one, not even Johnny, knew she was here. There was nothing sexual in their relationship, but only conversation. They spent a good majority of their time simply talking, discussing their lives and how they had intersected. The night before, he'd broken down while speaking with her, his voice thick with sobs, as he begged her forgiveness for keeping her here. She'd forgiven him and he felt cleaner, a feeling he enjoyed. It was an unstated fact that she could not leave knowing his true identity.

He touched her shoulder, "Susan?" She stirred under his touch. Her eyes fluttered open and she smiled up at him. "Would you like something to eat?" he asked her.

She stretched and yawned. "No. Not yet." She shook her head to get the sleep out of it.

Ezekiel watched as she struggled to wake up. "Something Mike said when he dropped you off that day at my office has been nagging at my mind." He rubbed a hand over his face. This seemed like a delicate conversation to have. "He said he ran you by the post office before bringing you here."

"Yes, I wanted to send a letter to my friend."

"A friend? You had been held prisoner, managed to escape, and you wanted to send a letter to a friend?"

"He's a cop in Kansas. I came through there and stayed a few weeks, but the people in the area kind of ran me off. Tom brought me down here. He said if I ever needed anything just send him a letter and he would come."

This news really shattered Ezekiel. Numbness crept into his limbs and he stared at the young woman. "You sent a letter to a cop in Kansas?"

"Sure, but it's been several days and he hasn't come for me."

"Did you tell him you were at Johnny's house?"

"I didn't know where I was. I just told him I'd been held against my will and he needed to come. I planned on being somewhere he could find me."

Ezekiel nodded and thought for a few silent moments about this.

Susan interrupted the silence. "I have a question for you. And I want you to tell me the truth."

He dipped his head, indicating he was listening. At first their relationship had been strained; he was, after all, keeping her locked in his basement. But with time, she could tell he meant her no more harm and little by little, the two had begun to trust each other, even to like each other. Actually, Ezekiel looked forward to her company, to her conversation every day.

"Will you tell me what happened to her? To Mary?"

He sucked in a deep breath through his nostrils. The story of Mary was one he had not shared with anyone. He never spoke of her, except that one day with Robert. Her presence had stayed with him, haunted him.

"We got started on this, this whole bootlegging thing, and at first, it was with pure intentions. But don't ever let anyone try to convince you that doing something sinful with pure intentions isn't still sin. I was too scared and naive to see it at that point." He sighed, reliving those early days as the Baptist preacher. "Mary was in charge back then. She ran the operation with the whole intention of saving the church. We did save the church and had many fights about whether or not we should give up bootlegging. It's difficult when a woman finds something to do, something that makes her happy, and is faced with giving that up. Well, she wouldn't.

"I did my best to ignore it. This was the first rift in our relationship, and as it would turn out, the only. I didn't know how to handle it. She'd become so independent. I began to rely on a family friend, Lucy, for support. She has problems with her spouse and so we could spend some time talking about the pain of marriage." He paused to run a hand through his hair. It wasn't that he never thought of Mary; it was that he never spoke about this.

"Lucy and I began to develop feelings for each other. It was difficult not to when she was around a lot helping with the church and the secret business, and it seemed that Mary was never around. And if she was, we'd fight about bootlegging. I never gave serious thought to leaving Mary. It was simply unheard of for a preacher to be divorced. I would have been run out of town from the church I'd sacrificed so much for. But Lucy talked a lot about leaving Mike. Her son, Robert, was only a few years old when I came to town, and she liked the idea of getting him away from his father.

"You have to understand that I still love Mary more than anything else in the whole world. But I am a sinful man, and I did not keep my guard up."

Susan placed a hand on his hand, and the warmth from it spread through Ezekiel's whole body. He felt calmed by her presence and took a moment to soak it up.

Ezekiel continued, "Our affair began during my third year here. Lucy was timid and gentle. I felt myself falling in love with her, a love that I still have to this day." He laughed without humor. "It is difficult to imagine that someone could love two women, but I do. Still to this day, I do.

"When Mary's body was found north of town, beyond the House, beyond the railroad tracks, I was completely obliterated. I felt like my life had come completely apart and the God I'd once taken complete faith in suddenly seemed to have left. It was ruled a suicide."

Susan stared into his eyes, waiting for more. When none came, she asked the question he'd hoped she wouldn't. "But why would Mary kill herself?"

"I've asked myself that same question for years. I'm not certain that she did. However, there isn't enough interest in her death for police to want to investigate it. Even when I'd taken over and paid the cops, none of them could find much other than suicide. She'd left a note out there. It looked like she'd walked out north of town with a small caliber gun and shot herself in the temple. I've never been able to accept that, but I have no proof that she didn't`.

"The note mentioned a lot of things, but said nothing of Lucy, so I like to believe that she didn't know about us, if she did indeed write the note. With that bit of confidence, Lucy and I continued our affair. And I took over the bootlegging, the thing I wanted to end. I weeded out the competition and the empire became what it was until Inspector Baxter came to town."

He shook his head. "I am certain her death is my fault. If it wasn't for coming to this town, she would still be alive. If I'd known what would happen to her, I wouldn't have even married her."

Tears slipped silently down his cheeks as he finished the story and something warm blossomed in his heart. He felt free of the burdens of Mary's death for the first time ever. He realized he'd been blaming God all this time for something that was simply his own fault. He'd never thought of it that way before now.

The two sat in silence. Susan had not the words for him, and Ezekiel had no more to say.

The ringing of the doorbell from upstairs interrupted that silence.

****

Michael watched from the sidelines for years as Mary continued to grow her bootlegging operation. He wanted to rise up, wanted to take over for her, but she would not allow it. It enraged him that a woman might act in this unsavory manner, and yet he felt he could do naught about it.

But when a man named Ramsey approached him, he finally felt he could rise up in the world.

Ramsey was the biggest competition that Mary had in the town. She'd slowly weeded out the smaller competitors and even had Michael destroy a couple of stills in the town that kept some of the families wet. That forced even more business to come her way. But there was still Ramsey.

They met one night in his car, the streetlight burned away the shadows just twenty feet from the front bumper, but inside the car, the light could not touch. The only light came from the burning end of Ramsey's cigarette. He spoke to Michael, his voice sounding the way boots crunching through gravel sound.

"You work for the bitch?" Ramsey asked.

Michael didn't need a name as he'd often thought of Mary in that way. "I do."

He pulled air in through the cigarette, his next words full of smoke. "I've worked hard in this town, I've worked hard to identify her. It took time because I never thought a woman was capable." Another pull. "Now that I know, I must remove her as a threat to my business."

"I understand."

"I thought you might." He dipped the cigarette into the ashtray, knocking the gray from the end. "Whatever you need, I will provide. Once she is out of the way, together we can make more money than you've ever dreamed."

Michael loved the idea. He liked the notion of putting Mary in her place. He honestly liked Ezekiel and knew that if he was in charge, Michael probably wouldn't be having this conversation.

Days went by before he made his move. It was a simple plan of convincing Mary to come with him, come out beyond the railroad tracks. He wanted to show her a place that he thought would be good for a speakeasy. That much was true, of course. But all good lies are steeped in truth, and it worked.

"I'm impressed, Michael. This is a good area with few travelers. The building could easily be purchased. We could really be rolling in the money with a speakeasy." She turned back to him and found herself face to face with a revolver. "Michael?" she asked, voice trembling slightly.

"I hate to do it, Mary, but I got a really good offer. Plus, this is no place for a woman. You understand, right?"

Although clearly distraught, and who wouldn't be under such duress, Mary held her composure and not a single tear slid down her face. Michael had to hand it to her; she was tough.

"Michael, you can't do this. Who put you up to it? We can make it right, you and I, together."

Michael began to shake his head long before she finished the sentence. “It’s too late for that, Mary. If I didn’t go through with this after coming this far, you’d never trust me again. I would live in fear.”

“You don’t think my husband will come for you?”

“I don’t. I intend to make it look like a suicide. Already have the note written.” He held up a paper. It looked nothing like Mary’s handwriting, he knew, but who could say that a suicidal woman’s handwriting might not change?

“Michael, please, you have to let me go. I could give it up, I could stop making moonshine.”

Michael smiled, a smile full of respect for the woman’s work ethic, if not for the woman. “No, you couldn’t, Mary.”

She stood for a moment and sighed heavily. “No, you’re right. I couldn’t.” She’d had her arms up in self-defense, but with this realization, she let them drop.

“Go ahead, Michael.”

“Oh, and I no longer go by Michael. I’m using my middle name now. Johnny. I want to be called Wild Johnny.”

“Good luck with that, Michael.”

He moved the gun to the side of her head and pulled the trigger. The gunshot wasn’t that loud, but it seemed to echo through the hills in Johnny’s head. He watched her body fall, watched her last breaths, and he stood there, trying to deal with the fact that he had taken a woman’s life.

He rubbed the handle of the gun in his shirt and placed it in her hand. He would need to burn these clothes and shower, but he’d done the job he had come to do. Now he could watch how things would play out.

Chapter 47

Nigel

Crime in the town appeared to be on the downhill trend, but Inspector Nigel Baxter still felt there was a piece he was missing. He'd gone over the details multiple times and come up short each time. His eyes remained unfocused as he stared past the room in front of him, attempting to find clues in what he had yet to discover.

He wanted to solve the puzzle since the governor had announced that the vote would be coming in the next couple of weeks on April 7. He didn't want the vote to come and go without any resolution to this problem. He'd been sure he would be able to get the young Australian to talk, but so far, had had nothing from him.

A knock at the door brought his attention back to his office and the pile of papers on his desk. Grant, a young officer new to the force, stood in the doorway, waiting with a rapt eagerness to get Nigel's attention. Beside Grant stood a man that Nigel didn't recognize. He held himself like an officer but didn't wear a uniform.

"Uh, sir? This is Tom Randolph. He's from Dodge City and would like to speak with you."

"Sure," Nigel said and waved a hand at the empty chair across from him. He waited for Tom to sit, but the man stayed in the doorway as if he couldn't muster the strength to walk that far. Finally Nigel peered up at him and said, "What is it you need?"

The young man shifted from one foot to the next. He cleared his throat. "I'm looking for someone."

Nigel smiled. "Aren't we all? You can file a Missing Persons down the hall." He paused. "But you already knew that, didn't you? Then why come to me?"

"You seem to be the most capable man here. No offense to the others."

Nigel nodded at him. "I'm sure none is taken."

"I brought a girl down here a few months back. We continued to correspond. Then her letters stopped. And out of the blue," he held up a wrinkled envelope, "I got this. In this letter, things have changed. She was in dire need of rescue. I came looking for her."

Nigel extended his hand and took the letter. He pulled the paper out and read the words. Clearly, the girl didn't know where she was when she wrote this, giving little in the way of clues. But something about it chimed deep in the inspector's brain. "How did she mail this?"

"What?"

"How did she mail this? If she's being kept prisoner as she says, surely her captor did not mail this for her?"

"I can't say that that is a possibility."

"So what happened? Did she escape? Is rescue no longer necessary?"

Tom Randolph stepped into the room then and sat on the edge of the chair. "But if she escaped, surely she would have contacted me in some way to let me know. It's been days since she sent that. I had to take vacation time to get down here." Desperation poured out with each word.

Nigel, still staring down at the letter, nodded. "I

believe you're right. She escaped, managed to mail the letter, then she, what? Got captured again?"

The young officer nodded. "Listen, I'm the one who brought her down here. I didn't stand up for her when my town cried out against her and wanted her gone. I'm the one. And I'm here to make that right. If something bad has happened to her, it's my fault and I can't live with that. Surely you can help me?"

The inspector sat in silence, taking slow, deliberate breaths. He made a decision as his eyes followed the curves of the letters within the letter. He felt each word, felt as if he watched the panicked girl write them. He knew he couldn't turn down this desperate man.

"I'll help you look for her." He dropped the letter, nodded. "It may not take priority, but I'll help you."

The young officer's face broke out into a smile that made him look even younger than he had. "Thank you, sir. Any idea where to start?"

"None, but that doesn't mean anything."

He pulled a small notebook toward him and began to jot a few notes when Officer Grant entered the office again. "Inspector, the Australian is ready to talk."

Nigel dropped the pencil and jolted to his feet. "I apologize, Mr. Randolph, I must run. I will be back with you shortly."

He didn't await the young officer's response, but bolted out of the door and down the hall to find Charles King and the final chapter of his tenure in the small town.

Chapter 48

Ezekiel

He didn't know what he expected when he answered the door. It wasn't unusual for someone from the church to swing by and talk, but after his last couple of sermons, he wasn't sure he could inspire anyone anymore. Or it could have been the police. There was a chance, he hoped a minute one, that Charles King would spill what he knew about Ezekiel. Filled with apprehension, Ezekiel opened the door.

Instead of policemen and flashing lights, he found a smile he'd been trying to forget that he missed. "Lucy," he said, swinging the door wide. "What brings you here?"

She stepped into the opened doorway and wrapped her arms around Ezekiel. "I've missed you. I don't know what I was thinking."

He reached for her, pulling her into his body, the smell of her perfume enveloping them. "I've missed you," he said, his voice coming out in a husky whisper. "I didn't realize how much until this moment."

Their lips found each other, meeting across the desire of days apart. In her kisses, he found what his lips missed more than a drowning man's lungs miss the taste of air. The kissing ended when Ezekiel's tears could no longer be ignored. Lucy stepped back, brushing the moisture from her skin as she stared at him. "What's wrong, Ezekiel?"

Tentatively, he touched his cheeks. He sighed upon finding the tears there. "I wish I could tell you. I've been feeling, well, actually *feeling* for the first time in years. I've come back to the land of the living."

"What do you mean?" Her hand trembled as she reached for him.

He cleared his throat. "Lucy, my dear, if you'll allow me. I'm in love with you. I'm not a good man, nor have I been for a very long time. I've been living this double life, maybe a triple life if you count our affair. And I don't want it anymore. I want you, that much is clear, and you being here, that proves that you want me, too."

She stepped back into him. "Of course I want you. Mike has been miserable to be around since Robert came home. Under normal circumstances, I'd like to think he'd be happy to be a grandfather, but the way he's been acting, I'm not so sure anymore. He scares me, Ezekiel."

"Let's put that behind us. Since you've come back to me, I'll turn in my resignation to the church this week, and I'll pack up. We'll leave town, go where the scandal can't follow us." He shrugged. "Or won't affect us. Maybe New York."

She smiled. "I'll go anywhere with you. Let me start packing, too."

He embraced her again, pressing her heart to his so that she could feel the love pumping through it. Everything would be just fine, he finally felt that, but at that moment, Susan began to scream.

Chapter 49

Ezekiel

Ezekiel met Lucy's eyes, his widening into great orbs, hers barely registering what she heard. His arms fell away from her, the memory of the captive in his basement suddenly coming back to him. "I, uh, need to run downstairs," he managed to say.

"Ezekiel, what was that?" Lucy asked.

Susan screamed again. Ezekiel raised an eyebrow. "I don't know what you mean."

Lucy stared at him then moved past him to the basement door. He followed her, pictured pushing her down the stairs, but knowing he never could. She walked down the stairs. He followed her. Lucy stared into the sparsely furnished room at the young woman sitting on the chair. "Help," Susan said, in a voice tattered from the screams.

Lucy turned with the speed of a three-legged turtle. "Ezekiel, who is she?"

Ezekiel stepped into the room to stand between the two ladies. He glared at Susan but turned to face Lucy with a smile. "She's a youth who's fallen on hard times. I've been letting her stay here, but for some reason she feels she's being held prisoner." Even as he spun the story, he realized he was furthering his triple life. If he couldn't be honest with her now, would he ever be able to?

"There's a girl living in your basement?"

"Yes, but I promise that nothing has happened between us." He hesitated for a moment. "Lucy, she knows *everything*."

Lucy's eyes grew yet again, taking in the wonder of it all.

Susan said, "I just can't stay here anymore."

Ezekiel turned back to her. "Susan, this is Lucy. She's come back to me, and I promise you that we'll let you go. Soon."

Tears filled Susan's eyes and slipped down her cheeks.

Lucy didn't seem to know what to say. Finally, she cleared her throat. "I'm pleased to meet you, Susan. I just wish I could understand what in the world is happening."

"All I wanted was a new life," Susan said, not quite crying, but tears falling down her face nonetheless. "I came to the Godforsaken Bible Belt hoping to start anew, and instead what I've found is judgment and treatment nearly worse than I had it back home. I thought I was finally going to get out of here, I thought I'd found help, but this preacher here is more worried about himself than anyone else. I said I wouldn't tell anyone as long as I can get out of here."

"And I said I would help you. It just isn't safe right now."

Lucy sat on the edge of the bed where Susan had slept. Though she wasn't tied up at all, the doors to the basement required a key to lock and unlock from both sides. It was something Ezekiel installed in case any parishioners stopped by. She reached for Susan's hand and held it. "Where can I take you?" Lucy asked. Susan seemed surprised at the idea that Lucy would want to help her. But this didn't surprise Ezekiel. It was one of the things he loved about Lucy, her desire to do good.

"I sent a letter to a policeman friend of mine, but I don't know if he got it. I would like to try to find him."

Lucy nodded. "Well, if I was in a strange place and needed help, I would go to the place that I'm the most familiar with."

"You think he's at the police station?" Ezekiel asked. That made a lot of sense, and he felt his heart swell a little more for Lucy.

"I could see that," Susan said. "Yeah, that's probably where he is."

Ezekiel's heart raced. Lucy was implying they should take a woman who knew all of his secrets to the police station. The thought really scared him. "We can't take her there." His voice came out in a hoarse whisper. Lucy turned to him, her mouth slightly parted.

"Ezekiel." The voice that spoke his name was soft and sweet, but it wasn't Lucy's. He turned to Susan. "You've shown me nothing but kindness while here. Really, you've given me food, a bed, and good conversation. I never felt like a prisoner here. Please, I just want to find my officer, and I want to get out of this town. For what it's worth, I won't say a word about you, unless it is to tell of your charity."

Lucy reached out and grabbed hold of Susan's hand. "You're a kind soul, Susan."

Susan smiled and held on to Lucy's hand as if it were the rope keeping her from drowning.

Ezekiel faced the two of them. Life had taken a funny turn recently, and suddenly, for the first time since the death of his Mary, he wanted to do the right thing. He filled his lungs full of air, held it, then released it in a gust. The oxygen flowed right into his brain and made everything seem clearer.

"All right, then. Susan, Lucy will take you down to the police station. Maybe you'll find your man. I hope so. If not, I suppose you could walk in there and tell Inspector Nigel Baxter who I am. He'll probably reward you greatly."

"Don't say that, Ezekiel," Lucy said. "She's not going to. She just told us that."

Ezekiel waved a hand. "I know. But I'm just saying I understand if she wants to." His shoulders slumped and his head fell forward so that his chin rested on his chest.

He sat like that while Lucy and Susan got ready to leave. Susan showered so that she would smell nice for her cop, assuming she would find him. The two of them chatted, and all the while, Ezekiel sat and thought about the past, the future, and his God damn present. He wished he could be past this and know the outcome. Like if this was a book, he would skip to the end to see how things turned out so he could make the right decision.

At last, it was time for Susan to leave. Ezekiel stood, but he didn't hug her. He didn't think that would be fair to her. But before she left she did meet his eyes. "I won't turn you in to the police, Ezekiel, but I can't make that promise about Johnny. I'd like to see him burn."

Ezekiel held her gaze and pictured life without Johnny. "That sounds like a fair trade to me, Susan. He deserves to burn for what he did to you."

Ten years melted from her face when she smiled. It was only then that you could actually tell how young she was. Lucy wrapped her arms around him, and whispered, "I'm going home to pack a bag. It's time, Ezekiel.

Tonight, we have to leave."

He had nothing to say to that. It was what he wanted to hear and what he hoped she would say. "I'll see you soon, then. I'll be ready."

Chapter 50

Nigel

Nigel took a breath before opening the door. Charles King was the key, he was sure, to ending this whole thing. The bed he'd been sleeping on these past few weeks was fine, but there was nothing like sleeping in your own space. How he longed for home, and how close he suddenly felt to it.

The Australian sat behind the table, staring down at his cuffed hand, a cigarette smoldering between his fingers. The smoke curled up around his head, blurring the very edges of his countenance. He did not look up when Nigel Baxter stepped into the room.

Nigel sat in his chair across from Charles and simply waited. His skin tingled with anticipation, and he wanted to scream, however, years of police work had taught him patience beyond that of nearly all men.

Without looking up, without even shifting his eyes, Charles began to speak, "The times I've had in this country are some of the best of my life. That's the only reason I'm willing to say anything. You can't take this away from me.

"I won't give you much, but I'll give you enough. How about that?"

Now Charles did look up to meet Nigel's eyes. "I need the head, Charles, I won't take anything less."

Charles scoffed. “Might as well send me on, then. I’ll be as good as dead if I give you that name.”

Nigel waited, sitting across from this Australian, this known criminal and wondered what chance he could take. Another name might lead him yet another step closer. And yet, another name meant more work, work that he’d grown tired of doing. He sighed and rubbed that lovely spot on the bridge of his nose that somehow eased the growing tension in his head. At last he said, “All right, here’s what I’ll do: I will cut you loose today, you can pack up and leave town, and tomorrow, I’ll make my move. That gives you nearly eighteen hours to work with.”

Before he even finished speaking, Charles had already started to shake his head. “It won’t work,” he said. “Do you think they’re not watching this place right now? They would see me leave, and I wouldn’t survive the afternoon. The man you’re after would be gone before nightfall, and the plan you just outlined would be voided.”

Nigel could feel it all slipping peacefully away. This was about all he had. There weren’t really any other leads, and this one had accidentally fallen into his lap. He decided he couldn’t ask for much more.

“I guess I don’t have a lot of choice.”

“I guess you don’t.” Charles leaned back, not quite smiling. “I’ll give you the name, the only one I’ll give, and then, after you arrest him, I want freedom. I’ll leave town, I’ll even leave the state, but I will never leave this country.”

Nigel didn’t say anything to this; it wasn’t necessary. He would probably let this man go, but he didn’t need to say it. He waited.

At long last, Charles spoke. "The next man up the food chain is Johnny Tompkins. He sometimes calls himself Wild Johnny."

Nigel leaned into the table, pulled his notebook from inside of his jacket pocket, and wrote the name down. "Where can I find him?"

Charles King smiled. "I told you I'd give you a name, and I have. But I won't be giving you anything else."

"Fine," Nigel said and stood. "I'll cut you loose, but not today. Hell, maybe not even tomorrow. You can sit for a few days while you think about how you treat your friends."

Nigel stepped out of the room, ignoring the protests of the prisoner.

He called for the attention of the other officers and held up the notebook. "I have a name. Not *the* name, but closer. So much closer. Gentlemen, if we play our cards right we could be finished with this today. Now someone tell me who Wild Johnny Tompkins is and where I can find him."

Chapter 51

Robert

In the quiet room of the quiet house, the pen scratched across the surface of the paper, an ingratiating sound like a mouse might make inside of a wall. The ink bled into the paper as words poured out of the pen. Each word, deliberate. Each spot on the paper, full of purpose and meaning. Robert sat behind his desk, constructing an eloquent goodbye letter with his Esterbrook ballpoint pen.

He'd deliberately left his father's name off the greeting, planning on leaving it for his mother while Mike was out. He didn't suspect that this would keep his dad out of the letter, but it would make an impact on him when he did find it, hopefully after his mother found it.

Robert had debated on leaving a note, but in the end had decided his mom, at the very least, deserved some sort of explanation. And he intended to explain everything.

"Dear Mom," he'd written, "By the time you read this, I'll be gone. I want you to know it's nothing you did. I can no longer stand this house or the man who pretended to be my dad."

His ribs ached, the bruises from Mike's boots screaming out at him, reminding him why he had to write this. Maybe Robert should have closed his mouth, but he still could not believe men who claimed to be as Godly as Mike Arrington could beat their own sons in the same way. No matter what he said or did, Robert believed that no son deserved that.

"I miss Becky," he continued to write. "I've thought of little else in the days since she left. I keep thinking that I helped create the child growing in her and I'm not going to abandon that. If Mike Arrington taught me anything, it was how to be a good father by being the opposite of him."

He relaxed his hand and stared at the wall in front of his desk. Tacked to it was a single sheet of paper, the only letter he'd received from Rebecca Lewis since she'd moved. She'd written four sentences: "I miss you. I love you. Come soon. I love you." He stared at it every day and pictured her writing it to him. In his mind he could see the swell of her belly as the baby grew inside of her. He could nearly imagine what it would be like to lay his hands on that belly and feel his baby move.

He picked up his pen again. "I have to confess that this was not the life I pictured for myself. I never intended to start drinking or to have premarital relations. I thought the preacher would help me, that's why I agreed to visit him, but he didn't. And in a way, this really is his fault."

Robert's heart skipped. He hadn't intended on writing that. His thoughts had gotten away from him and he'd laid it out there. If he'd written it in pencil, he would have erased it. As it was, he didn't have any other sheets of paper, so he decided to leave it. And expound on it.

"Every struggle I've had, instead of helping me through them, he encouraged me to experience them. And maybe a lot of bad came from my meetings with

Brother Ezekiel, but I still believe that some good came from them.

"And, Mom, I have to tell you, I know about your affair. It wasn't something I wanted to know or sought out. I accidentally overheard a conversation that was meant to be private. I won't tell Mike, but maybe you should. I'd like to see you happy."

He took a shaky breath, rested his hand, and then continued.

"I am in love with Rebecca Lewis and our unborn child. I'm going to climb in the work truck and head north to her. I won't be finishing high school. I don't even know what I'll be doing to make a living, but I can't stand by and believe that the God you've taught me to worship all these years would be satisfied with me abandoning my child."

His earliest memory of church was not one of happiness as his parents would like to think it was. Church was boring, always, and he found that he had trouble sitting and standing and sitting again. He would fidget and get a thump to the back of the head. He associated church early on with pain and boredom. Not a lot had changed in the last few years. He'd found some enjoyment in youth group, but going to "big church" as they called it, still held no real value to him. God forbid he miss a Sunday morning, a Sunday night, or a Wednesday night of any given week. Though those were the only times his dad was fine with him not working.

"I hope that someday you can see that this was the best decision. I know Dad never will, but maybe you will. And maybe someday you can see your grandchild and forgive me of all these teenage transgressions. I love you."

He signed his name at the bottom of the letter and sighed. The writing wasn't as good because the cast got in the way, but the message was effective. He'd already packed his bags, two of them, and thrown them in the back of the truck. He pulled out his Buddy Holly record, the one he wasn't supposed to have and left it on the table by his mother's chair. He slid the letter inside the sleeve with the record. He grabbed a hat, his favorite, and popped it on his head. With the letter from Rebecca in hand, he walked out of his bedroom for the last time, ready to put some miles between himself and the only house he'd ever known as home.

Chapter 52

Nigel

Nigel Baxter approached the car with a gun drawn. Through the window he could see an inert figure sitting behind the wheel. "Wild Johnny," he called. There was no response from the man. As he got closer, he could see the blood. He tapped the window with the barrel of the gun, but there was no movement inside. "Johnny?" he called again and opened the door. The smell hit him down deep and jerked at his meager supper, trying to make it reappear. He stepped back and put his hands on his knees for a second, to recover. Finally, he trotted over to the other waiting officers and the ambulance. "Better get over there," he said to K.P. one of the EMTs on duty for the night. "It doesn't look so good."

Officer Grant came up beside Nigel and sighed. "This is the end, isn't it, boss?"

"Perhaps, Grant." Nigel popped a cigarette into the corner of his mouth and lit it. He hadn't needed the fuel of nicotine for several days now, but suddenly, he couldn't get enough of it. The smoke burned away the taste of bile at the back of his throat and sent his head soaring to the sky. He held up the cigarette and gazed at the burning end through one eye. "Here's something I can control. I can light it and feel as if my destiny is my own. That's why *he* did it." He pointed the cigarette at the car. "It was his last little bit of control of a life where he had lost all of it." He took another drag.

K.P. pulled Wild Johnny's body out of the car and onto the stretcher. The other EMT stepped forward to help with the legs. What was left inside of Johnny's head spilled onto the white sheet covering the stretcher. Nigel pulled a handkerchief from his pocket to cover his mouth. His eyes watered and he coughed to clear the taste of the smell from his throat. Beside him, Officer Grant fell to his knees and let loose a torrent of vomit.

"Cut that out, man," Nigel said, grabbing at his collar and pulling him back. "The last thing we need is a police officer vomiting all over a crime scene."

K.P. covered the body with a second white sheet and got it loaded up on the ambulance. Nigel snubbed out the end of his cigarette, rolled the butt into a ball, and placed it in his pocket. A cigarette butt wouldn't make much difference compared to the vomit pile beside him, but he still did not like to leave anything at a crime scene.

His eyes studied the car, the blood puddling in the seat, splashed harsh and crimson across the backseat and windows. Such carnage. No matter how many bodies he saw, he was always impressed with the thought that the fragile lives of man could be taken with the spilling of blood. How that liquid could be the representation of someone's thoughts and memories and experiences, Nigel could not quite grasp it.

Another officer, not Grant, came up beside Nigel. "Someone warned him."

Nigel nodded. "Probably." He shrugged. "It amounts to the same. He needed to do this, to take control. But it saves us a lot of time and money. I'm sure this is the end of the whole thing, aren't you?"

The officer nodded. "Johnny was probably the head of the whole thing. I've known the guy for a few years. I thought he was shady. We brought him in on a couple charges, but never anything that could stick. Certainly nothing like that Australian accused him of."

Nigel rubbed his cheek, his eyes refusing to leave the congealing blood. Charles King had finally talked, that was true. He'd given a name, and said it wasn't the top name. But surely this was the end.

And yet.

Something in his bones cried out that it wasn't over, not yet. He'd slowly arrested as many people connected to the illegal booze movement as he could. He'd cleaned up the police force and found the most corrupt of those in town. But something still hung on the air like the moisture after a summer storm.

It had taken them nearly an hour to find Johnny's car. He'd driven out to the north of town, just past that speakeasy they'd busted days earlier. It seemed like a place for solace and loneliness. The story Nigel had heard when they'd arrived was that it was the exact place where the Baptist preacher's wife had killed herself. He hadn't known she'd committed suicide.

He wiped at his face with the handkerchief and tried to shake the feeling. "See if there's anything useful in the car," Nigel said to the officer standing next to him.

"Huh?"

"It was the last place he was alive." Nigel spoke slowly out of annoyance. "There could be something important in there."

The young officer did not appear happy to go pawing through the inside of the car caked with the dead man's blood, but Nigel didn't care. He'd ranked up so he didn't have to be the one traipsing through blood. He'd done enough of that in his younger days in Chicago.

He watched with interest as the cop looked under the driver's side seat, and finding nothing, went around to the other side of the car. He tried the glove box but found it locked.

"Get the keys," Nigel yelled at him. Reluctantly, the young officer reached across the car to take the keys out of the ignition. He popped the key into the glove box and clicked it open. Inside was a white envelope. The officer lifted the envelope and held it up for Nigel to see. Nigel held out his hand.

Slowly the officer backed out of the car. Nigel could see a bit of blood had soaked into his uniform as he walked over to Nigel and placed the envelope in the inspector's hand. Nothing was written on it. Nigel slid a finger under the seal and opened it. Inside he found a folded sheet of paper.

To whom it may concern:

My name is Michael Jonathan Tompkins. I'm a resident of this damn town, and I've found trouble in my life. During the last fourteen years, I've been a dealer in illegal booze in and around the area. I've committed arson, murder, disposal of bodies, and any other number of things, most recently, kidnapping. I'd like to think you're here because of the the girl I kidnapped who escaped from me. But probably you're here because of Charles.

Nigel Baxter, if you're reading this, I am not who you're looking for. But you're close.

There's one more rung on the ladder above me. Look for him where dancing and drinking are not allowed, but happen anyway. All I ask of you is to keep my name out of the papers; I wouldn't want my mother to be disappointed in me.

Sincerely,

Wild Johnny Tompkins

Nigel read and re-read the letter, taking careful time with the clues that Johnny offered as to who he needed to look for next. It didn't make a ton of sense to him. The young officer was still standing next to him. "Any idea where dancing and drinking wouldn't be allowed but happen anyway?" Nigel asked the man.

The officer glanced at the paper then back up at Nigel. He chuckled. "Sounds like a Baptist joke to me."

"Baptist?" The word sent a cold shiver down Nigel's spine, but he wasn't quite ready to think about that.

"Sure. They are very outspoken on dancing and drinking, but they all do it. Everyone knows at least one Baptist who would tell you not to drink while they have alcohol on their breath. It's just a joke," he added, seeing the look on Nigel's face.

Something sinister snaked its way into Nigel's mind. A voice rang out through his ears, a voice cursing drinking and over and over in his mind, he saw the preacher standing behind the pulpit calling out the sins of his flock. Nigel's heart jumped into overdrive. "I have to go," he said. He sprinted back to his car and sped off toward the First Baptist Church.

Chapter 53

Ezekiel

Guilt was a funny thing. Ezekiel had murdered, sold an illegal substance to addicts, had an affair with one of his deacon's wives, and kept a woman in his basement against her will. And yet through all of that, he'd maintained a clear conscience, giving up on a God he'd so vehemently believed in during his younger days.

He didn't know what it was, whether it was the conversations with Susan or the slow bleed of his booze empire, but something had brought back his feeling of guilt, his desire to do good. Maybe it was love. Maybe he could have a life, a normal life, with Mike Arrington's wife.

After Lucy left with Susan, he stayed in the haunted house by himself. He packed up what he thought he would need so he'd be ready when Lucy got back. He still felt a sting in the corners of his eyes thinking of the phone call he'd gotten just moments after Lucy had left with Susan.

"Hello?" He'd clutched the receiver, expecting to hear Lucy's voice.

"Boss, it's Johnny. I've just gotten word from a secretary down at the police station. They've called everyone in. It seems Charles is going to talk. Maybe he already has."

The preacher let the news sink in. “Okay, Johnny. That’s fine.”

“Fine?” His voice came out louder than necessary. “How can it be fine? I’m freaking out. There are only two people he could name and I doubt he’ll name you. And if he did, who would believe him?”

“Calm down, Johnny. Maybe he won’t say anything. They’ve just tried to scare him. Maybe he’s trying to get their hopes up for no reason. We’ve trained him. Do we need to worry?”

“I have to tell you…” Johnny breathed into the phone.

“Yes, Johnny, what is it?”

“Your wife, Mary?”

Ezekiel’s heart jumped into overtime at the mention of Mary. “What about her?”

Johnny took another breath, the wind of it rushing over the phone receiver like wind from a cave. “She didn’t kill herself.”

“Oh, Johnny, I’ve always thought that, but there’s nothing to suggest—“

“I killed her, Ezekiel. It was me. I thought I could take over, I would be the man. But then you stepped in and I couldn’t…well, I’m just sorry.”

Ezekiel couldn’t think of what to say, but it didn’t matter; Johnny had hung up.

He stared at the phone in his hand and watched as that hand replaced the phone in its rightful place. He’d never really believed that Mary had killed herself, always held onto the idea that she was stronger than that, and now, he knew the truth. He wanted to rush out the door, right then, and rip Johnny Tompkins to shreds. He wanted to hold his head over his wife’s grave and see if the blood of her killer might revive her. He'd wanted to, but then he didn't.

Ezekiel figured that Johnny would go out in a hail of bullets, taking as many cops as he could with him. He could see that stupid coward, killing innocent people, just as he'd killed Mary.

He'd wanted to call Johnny back, but the phone felt too heavy in his hand. Instead, he paced the living room and tried to think. He could feel a breaking of his resolve; could almost hear the walls he'd built around his heart, breaking. "Sometimes," he'd once preached, "God will go to great lengths to get your attention. What will you do about it when He does?" It was a question he remembered asking in the pulpit once. Empty words, but now they echoed back across the days and weeks, and hit him in the gut.

Lucy called after dropping off Susan, so she was heading home to pack and would be back with him shortly. Their new life would start in a few short hours. He'd left his letter of resignation in the kitchen for whoever to find. And he'd waited.

With the memories of Mary, the truth of her murder, and the prospects of leaving it all behind haunting him, Ezekiel grabbed his Bible and cracked it open. He still read it every week, but only to find passages that backed up his sermons. Now, he opened it for answers. He skipped around a little, attempting to remember where the good stuff was, but it still didn't quite feel right, knowing there was a hidden room below him that housed a few jars of illegal hooch.

He lifted the heavy book and carried it out the door with him. Early April had been kind to the Okies so far, and today was no exception. That Saturday evening was a beautiful seventy-two degrees and was almost enough to keep the preacher outside. The prediction for rain later in the week had gotten his hopes up that maybe it would be enough to keep people from getting out to vote, but suddenly, he didn't really care. Nigel Baxter had done his job and done it well. It almost assuredly would pass and prohibition would end. Ezekiel sighed at the thought.

He made his way to the front of the church and opened the front door; he rarely locked it, hoping that any of his patrons could come in and pray if the Spirit moved them, as he himself had suddenly been moved.

He flipped on one of the lights in the sanctuary, the glow from it casting an eerie vestige around the room. Unlike his Baptist nature, he found a seat on the front row, and for a while he simply stared up at the stage, trying to visualize himself standing behind the cross-shaped pulpit. He sighed and opened the Bible again, this time finding the sixth verse in the thirty-first chapter of Deuteronomy. He read it aloud, "Be strong and of good courage, fear not, nor be afraid of them: for the Lord thy God, he it is that doth go with thee; he will not fail thee, nor forsake thee."

He reread it and felt a tremor run through his body. He wondered briefly if God could forgive him after all this time. He closed the Bible and stood, keeping his eyes on the cross-shaped podium. He could picture Christ hanging from it and tears slid from his eyes. "Am I so lost?" he uttered. "Have I forsaken you?"

In the depths of his soul, he knew it was true. He'd been the one to turn away when things got bad. It was his own mistakes and shortcomings that led to Mary's death, not God's. He saw that now, but after so many sins and transgressions, he didn't know how he could ever be forgiven.

He fell to his knees on the steps leading up to the pulpit. Suddenly he felt very unworthy to be in the presence of God. He opened his mind to Him for the first time in at least a decade. He fell into prayer as easily as falling into the ocean on a hot summer day. He stayed that way for quite some time and would have stayed that way maybe for the whole night if it hadn't been for the sanctuary door opening. He heard someone enter the room behind him.

His first thought was that Lucy had finally gotten away from her house and had come to take him away. But then Johnny's words came back to him about Charles confessing. It seemed quite possible then that the police had come for him. He raised his head at the sound, breaking off his stream-of-consciousness confession to find out who'd come in.

He stood and turned to face the door of the sanctuary. A lone man walked down the aisle in the shadows toward him. Ezekiel could make out the form of a man, but not who it was. He seemed too tall to be Nigel Baxter, but he couldn't think of who it would be. When the man stepped into the light, Ezekiel was surprised to see Mike Arrington. An unlikely fear crept up around his midsection at the sight of his head deacon.

"Hello, Mike. What brings you out tonight?"

Mike's eyes were ringed with red and tears spilled down from them. Ezekiel had seen Mike cry before, the man was in touch with his emotions, but he'd never seen him quite like this. His back was bent and he couldn't quite meet the preacher's eye. And his clothes were filthy. In the dim light, he seemed to be splattered with mud.

“I was just spending some time in prayer, Mike. We’ve got church tomorrow, you know?” Ezekiel attempted to get control of his heart rate. Mike had really startled him.

“Hmmm.” Mike stared at the ground as if he needed to memorize the fibers of the carpet. Ezekiel had spent a great deal of his life watching people and getting to know them. He’d known Mike better than almost anyone in town. He sensed that something had changed in the man, and he didn’t like it.

“Well, don’t be shy,” Ezekiel said after a moment, “come on in and pray with me. I’d enjoy the company.”

Mike’s gaze jumped around the room and his body started to shake. Finally he stepped closer to the preacher and Ezekiel could see that the splatter on his clothes was red, a crimson every Christian knows as the color of spilled blood.

“Mike? Are you all right? Did you have an accident?”

Mike looked down at the blood on his shirt and for the first time, met the preacher’s eyes. “I killed her.”

Ezekiel’s heart had so nearly recovered from the scare of Mike coming in but now it burst into full speed again. “Killed who, Mike?”

“Lucy. I murdered my wife.” He reached behind his back and pulled a gun from the waist of his jeans. He kept it at his side. “I shot her. She’s dead, Pastor.”

Ezekiel wanted to scream and cry. What could drive the man to do such a thing? He kept himself composed and took a step forward. “Okay, Mike, walk me through what happened.” He stuck out his hand. “And start by handing me the gun.”

Mike made no move to do that. Instead he kept his

eyes on the preacher while he lifted his left hand. Clutched in it was a piece of paper. “Robert’s gone, but he left a letter. Lucy was supposed to find it. But I found it first. I could have screamed when I found a Buddy Holly record in my living room. When I threw the record, the letter fell out.”

Ezekiel’s brow crinkled. “A letter? What does it say?”

“ ‘I know about your affair.’ He explains that he overheard my wife and my preacher. What do you think he means by that?”

Ezekiel rubbed his head, feeling as if he’d just been punched. “Mike, can we talk about this?” He couldn’t believe Robert had been so stupid, leaving evidence like this. He knew his father was always a little on edge.

“He also says that it was you.” Mike pointed a finger at the preacher with the hand clutching the letter. “It was you who encouraged his rebellious behavior. I sent him to you so that he would stop that nonsense. And you made it worse.” Mike’s face turned bright red, his eyes bulged and spit flew from his raging mouth. “I trusted you! You took everything from me. I have no wife, my son has taken off, and even my church that was always my safe haven is gone. And it’s your fault!”

He lifted the gun, pointing it at his preacher. Ezekiel held up a hand; he’d been on the wrong end of a gun before, but he’d always had the upper hand. “Mike, you don’t want to do this. Not in the Lord’s house.”

“Do not speak to me of the Lord.” He shifted his arm and fired a bullet into the podium. A chunk of wood exploded out of the cross. “God is dead.”

“No, Mike, don’t say that. Don’t blame the shortcomings of man on God.”

He brought the gun back to the preacher and stared down the barrel at him. “You’re still preaching to me? Even after all you’ve done?”

“Listen to me, Mike.” His eyes filled with tears and his voice quaked. “I’ve made mistakes, and I will be punished for it. But you can’t be the one. I can’t let you go to Hell because of my mistakes.”

“I’ll meet you there,” he said and pulled the trigger. The bullet tore out of the barrel and thudded into the preacher’s chest. It nicked his heart before passing through his back. Ezekiel Wilson fell to the ground, his hand grasping at the wound in his chest. His eyes darted from the gunman to the cross-shaped podium. The light shining around it looked miraculous to his dying eyes.

“Lord, forgive him,” Ezekiel whispered. “He knows not what he does.” Blood spilled out of him with each beat of his broken heart. He smiled as he thought of seeing Mary again, seeing Lucy again, of finding his eternal resting place.

Ezekiel stared up at Mike, not seeing him, but seeing eternity all around him. His lungs pulled one last breath, and as it flowed out of his body, so did his soul.

Epilogue

On April 7, 1959, the good people of Oklahoma voted to end prohibition in the state for good, though it would take another sixty years before people voted to loosen some of the conservative liquor laws and eradicate the existence of low-point (non-intoxicating) beer in the state.

Nigel Baxter celebrated with his fellow officers then left town, heading home for the first time in months. The governor was so deeply impressed with his work that Nigel had his own office at the state capitol. Still the events of Saturday night haunted the veteran cop to the point that he was considering retirement.

He'd been on the front porch of the preacher's home, knocking on the door, when he heard the first gunshot, the one that had splintered the podium. By the time he got into the church, the second shot had been fired, the shot that killed Ezekiel Wilson. Nigel hadn't saved the preacher, but he had saved Mike from himself, wrestling the gun away from the murderer's forehead.

After Mike was in custody, they found the body of his wife at his house. They also searched the preacher's home and found the secret room in the basement. Nigel remembered all the conversations he'd had with the preacher that had hinted at the behavior he found evidenced in the man's house, but he still could not quite believe it. Ezekiel Wilson had never struck him as a bad man, but maybe he'd been that good at faking it.

On the Monday night before the vote, Robert Arrington, having no idea of the doom of his parents, arrived at Rebecca's aunt's house. The reunion had been among the most joyous things the two of them had ever shared. It was the memory and the strength of the girl he loved that kept him strong after he learned of his mother's murder.

Robert kept all of his promises to Rebecca and the ones he'd made in the letter to his mother. He cared for the girl and their baby daughter who was born that November. Although he still felt a love for Oklahoma and the home he'd left behind, Robert didn't go back for a long time. Even through his dad's trial and sentencing. He felt he had no reason, and Rebecca wasn't excited to ever see her parents again after they'd sent her away. It was nearly thirty years before he took his family back through the area. He showed his two daughters and three sons, his sons-in-law, and his two grandkids the place he'd called home and the place where he'd fallen in love with their mother.

At the cemetery, he found his mother's final resting place, the first and only time he would see it in his life. Mike Arrington was not buried. After his execution, he was cremated by the state. However, Ezekiel Wilson was buried near his mother and something about that comforted Robert. The preacher was, after all, partly responsible for his relationship with Rebecca.

He left that town for the last time in 1987, content to never think about it again. Rebecca passed away in 2011 due to complications from a heart attack she suffered earlier in the year. Robert, always the romantic, followed her to the grave a month later at the age of seventy.

A word about the author…

Nicholas Lyon is a father, husband, teacher, wood turner, musician, and writer. He discovered his love for writing during a Creative Writing class in college taught by the incendiary Dr. Jim Yates. Since then, he's completed three novels and multiple short stories and won several awards for writing. Currently, he teaches high school English, and is the Public Relations Director for Oklahoma Writer's Federation, Inc. He lives in Oklahoma with his wife, two boys, two dogs, and one cat.

Thank you for purchasing
this publication of The Wild Rose Press, Inc.

For questions or more information
contact us at
info@thewildrosepress.com.

The Wild Rose Press, Inc.
www.thewildrosepress.com

www.ingramcontent.com/pod-product-compliance
Lightning Source LLC
Chambersburg PA
CBHW060534260626
47161CB00003B/897

* 9 7 8 1 5 0 9 2 4 5 9 9 4 *